DATING A PRO

NEVER TOO LATE
BOOK SEVEN

DONNA MCDONALD

VISIT DONNA'S WEBSITE

Cover by *LFD Designs for Authors*

Edited by *The Proof Is In The Reading*

ACKNOWLEDGMENTS

Thanks to my critique partner, Robyn Peterman, for being a surprising font of useful golf information.

College classes rock and everything counts when you're an author. You will be the reason for any literary hole-in-one I get.

Pun intended—Babe.

DEDICATION

For my college golf partner, Lisa Norwood.

I thought of you the whole time I was writing this book. I was never in your league, or anyone else's on the green, but I still think of our games that summer as one of the best times of my life. You were the epic good sport with my learning curve and I was your divot queen. Thank you for your tolerance and for the golf ballerina two-step assist when I zealously sent a chunk of manicured lawn flying.

ABOUT THIS ROMANCE

Sometimes you can't tell from a cover or blurb what a romance is about, how sexy it is, or if it's something you're going to want to read. If you land on this page in the sample, I hope this helps you make the decision to add this wonderful story to your romance collection.

The topics and themes found in this story encompass the following subjects:

steamy romance, happily ever after, HEA, romance over 40, secret baby, sports romance, romantic comedy, contemporary romance, later in life romance, romance over 30, rekindled romance, and more...

INTRODUCTION

Harrison Walter Graham was already in his eighties when I introduced him in DATING A SILVER FOX and DATING A COUGAR II. I loved Harrison's irreverent character from the moment he hit the page. Every time Harrison talked about his wife, the incomparable Doris, he reminded me of comedian George Burns telling stories about his wife, Gracie.

In DASF, Harrison pushed his friend, Lydia McCarthy, into giving Morrison Fox a chance. He repeated that a book later in DACII by pushing Morrie's daughter, Jane Fox, into giving his grandson, Walter, a chance. So I decided in this book, it was time to give Harrison a chance.

To do that, I had to wind back the writing clock to 1965 which for a contemporary author is practically like writing a historical. All I can say is thank heaven for the internet. I was in elementary school in 1965 so I remember that time, but I still had to do quite a bit of research.

Life changed daily in the sixties, but that change came slower to elite country club societies in historic towns. Anyone seen the movie *Dirty Dancing* which was set in 1963? That's exactly what I'm talking about. I hope you enjoy my little blast from the past.

Happy reading!
~ Donna McDonald

CHAPTER 1

Spring had fully sprung in 1965...

Having a legitimate partner was a hard and fast rule, not that Harrison cared all that much about rules, but it was one of the few he'd never tried to break. To use the pristine course with its green curvy paths, your golf partner had to also be a wealthy Falls Church Country Club member.

Cocky, young William McCarthy had been the only man available when he'd desperately wanted on the green. The kid was a newly finished college senior and thought he knew everything about everything. Of course, so had he at that age. At thirty-three Harrison did know a lot of things—things like how to go after what he wanted with a single-minded focus.

Today he was willing to tolerate playing golf with the devil if it meant he might catch sexy divorcee, Doris Isette Pearson, playing his favorite game. He'd had his masculine eye on the older woman for years, but that had been only lust and wishful thinking. Now dating her was legally possible. He even admired the fact that the successful Falls Church attorney had handled her own divorce. In it, Doris had done a bang-up job of making her ex-husband, Avery Vincent, look like the serial two-timer everyone knew he was.

Harrison was purposely here on Doris's typical day to visit the course. He'd been showing up on this day every week for nearly two months, trying to accidentally-on-purpose run into her. Having his fingers in too many entrepreneurial pies had made it a real challenge to be consistent. His timing had so far been off and he'd managed to often arrive just after she'd finished and gone home.

The fact irritated him mostly because he usually had better luck chasing a woman he was interested in the way he was interested in the Honorable *Ms.* Pearson, as she liked to be called. The woman was a brilliant, but frustrating, enigma in many ways.

It wouldn't surprise him one bit to hear Doris personally knew the *Ms.* term's strongest proponent, civil rights worker Shelia Michaels. He'd been unimpressed when he'd heard the woman speak about it on the radio a couple years ago. But what did Doris's title matter to him? The last thing he needed was some woman looking to one day be called *Mrs. Graham.* Doris's feminist leanings and independence were in the plus column for him.

"Heard your old man just got married for the fifth time, Graham. My father's in awe because he says yours has never lost his club membership to any dame he kicked to the curb. Guess you're happy about that too. I also heard your father didn't get saddled with alimony payments big enough to affect his finances. You're the son of a real genius. No wonder you're so good at making money."

"What happened wouldn't have mattered to me either way," Harrison said, narrowing his gaze as he studied the younger man more closely. "I make all the money I'm ever going to need."

He also didn't give a damn about any of the women who married his father and tried to replace his dead mother. They were all destined to fail because his mother had been unique. Though his father hadn't treated her like she was, Harrison had always seen her specialness. He'd looked for it himself in every woman he met. His father's lack of success in finding someone like his mother mirrored his own.

William chuckled as he shrugged both shoulders. "Sure. I can buy into the whole self-made man thing, but you can never have enough family moola though, right? The Graham legacy is why you get to date so many of the rich babes."

"Fore!" Harrison yelled before his shot, even though he knew they were the only ones on the course. He was hoping to derail McCarthy's big mouth, which hadn't shut up gossiping since they reached the green. He smacked the white ball solidly, feeling a swish of wind on his follow-through. Man—he never got tired of that feeling. It was really the only reason he played.

After his shot fell and started to roll, Harrison turned to his golf mate and frowned at the comment. It was true that his father was a well-known philanderer, but most people had enough social graces not to directly point out family faults to him.

"Nice landing," William said.

"Thanks." Harrison's mouth twisted as he watched McCarthy tee up.

The impatient younger man took his swing hurriedly, and then swore at where his shot had gone. They both picked up their golf bags and started walking toward where his ball had stopped just a few feet from the hole. They were going to have to search the woods for McCarthy's. Hopefully, the man would do better as they moved along.

Harrison took his time lining up his easy shot. "I guess I don't feel the need to marry my fortune. Though I am a flagrant opportunist like my father, I honestly come to the club to play golf, not to find wealthy women to date. Dating someone here just works out for me sometimes."

He shook his head when McCarthy laughed as if he'd told a joke.

"Being a handsome bastard helps too, I imagine. You must

have gotten your looks from your mother's side. Like everyone else, I've noticed you pretty much date whoever you want, but what I find interesting is you never keep any of them. Every businessman needs a wife to help him build his career. I thought the great entrepreneur, Harrison Walter Graham, would have picked a proper showpiece already."

Harrison raised his head from the white ball he'd been pondering. "What's a showpiece? I'm patiently waiting for the perfect woman to cross my path. A smart-minded man looks for quality instead of quantity, McCarthy."

"Yes, but quantity is so much fun. Of course, bed partner consistency probably has its benefits too. And I'll admit it—I'm considering settling down. My parents are already pushing for grandchildren. Right now, I've got my eye on cute, little Lydia Smithfield."

Harrison knew the quiet girl and thought she deserved someone much better than William McCarthy. Unfortunately her parents never let the kid breathe on her own, much less date someone without money or a long-standing country club membership. Lydia was dragging her feet about dating, but like most females born into prominent Falls Church families, she'd likely cave to her parent's plans for her eventually. Not many young women had enough fight in them to buck the well-oiled machine of wealth and privilege.

"Why don't you pick someone to marry who might actually challenge you, McCarthy? Lydia's just a kid—a very *green* kid— and you know what I mean."

William laughed again, and Harrison knew his words of warning weren't worth the breath it had taken to say them aloud.

"I'm not an old man like you yet, Harrison. I like my women green. Lydia's legal and her still being a kid in most ways is perfect for my plans. You see, her parents are making her go to an all girls college, which will reduce my competition to nil. I'll have to dangle her along while she gets her degree, but that will leave me free for at least four more years to enjoy being a bachelor."

"What about loving her, William? Is that part of your master plan?" Harrison asked, watching the younger man play the ball that had they'd finally found beside a tree.

He didn't say anything when his partner tossed the ball a good three feet from the edge of the fairway before walking to it. William's smooth follow-through swing spoke of masculine confidence as he sent his cheated shot arcing through the air, but it was the younger man's conversation which betrayed his true nature.

"Are you seriously expecting to fall in love at your age? My father says that's not how it works for men with money. It may be 1965 everywhere else, but it's still 1955 here in Falls Church. My parents expect me to marry a decent girl and have a family. If I pick someone now, they'll leave me alone until my trust fund matures in three years. I figure by the time Lydia leaves college, I'll have sufficiently sown my wild oats. I'll be as good to her as any other husband would be."

Harrison grunted. "Will you? Your plans sound pretty calculating."

William laughed. "Why do you think I majored in business? My parents will approve of her... and therefore approve of me for marrying her."

Harrison snorted, having to work to hide his disgust. "Love isn't something you can plan. Maybe I'll die an optimist, but when I marry—*if* I marry—it will be to a woman I adore."

"You're a dreamer, Harrison. A dreamer. Your dreaming obviously works for you in business, but you should be a realist in the rest of your life. And by the way... I suck at golf and yet am ahead by more than three strokes. So who's the smart one?"

"Keep your shirt on, McCarthy. We're only on the third hole. You play the short game. I, on the other hand, do everything with the long-term in mind."

As they walked to the next hole, Harrison thought of all the nights he ate alone. Would he like to find a wife? Sure he would. But he'd been focused on his business and waited too long by country club standards. Good women tended to marry in their early twenties. Harrison figured it was so they never got tempted to be bad. All that were left unmarried by their mid-twenties were shy spinsters or widows, unless you had the gonads to take on a woman someone else had cast aside.

Personally? He liked divorced women for a tumble, but to marry one? That was never happening. His four stepmothers were no better than his father. They were already on husbands two, three, and... whatever.

His family history was enough reason for him not to get serious with a retread. But to get a woman no other man had screwed up, he'd have to marry someone at least a decade younger than him. Then he'd be stuck with a woman who had no sense of herself or the world.

He'd all but given up dating because he couldn't even handle dinner and a movie with anyone under twenty-five without getting bored. Court an eighteen year old like McCarthy kept talking about doing? That was a true kid by his over thirty standards.

Harrison would be the first to admit he hadn't lived like a monk until just recently, but years of experience had taught him you could only stay in bed a certain amount of time. Every year he got older, he longed more and more for someone who was also interesting outside the sheets. His risk-taking nature told him she was out there if he just kept looking hard enough.

The country club—and Falls Church—was full of east coast, ivy league educated women, and he'd dated several of them. Given those dating odds being present in his favorite hunting ground, sure—he'd been hoping to cull the herd sooner.

It was a sad situation when a successful man in his prime

couldn't find a woman he liked talking to for more than five minutes.

~

"HELLO, Ms. Pearson. I see you brought the divot queen back with you today. Want me to find you a spiked caddy to help mend the lawn as you go? Might keep your game moving a little faster."

"It won't work—not if the boy is even fractionally good-looking," Doris said dryly, grinning at her favorite greenskeeper before looking toward her niece, who was eyeing a new pale blue golf skirt. "Vivian, stop mooning and pick out your size. I'll get it for you. Bring it over here and let Lloyd ring it up with our fees."

The girl made happy sounds and started searching through the hangers. Doris smiled as she turned back. "Who's ahead of us today?"

"Just one set—McCarthy and Graham. Probably on the fifth hole about now," he reported.

Doris nodded. McCarthy wasn't a problem. Vivian had dated him and declared him an ass already. But Harrison Graham? He was a different sort of man, and you could never tell what was on his agenda. Her blonde, curvy, and attractive twenty-two-year-old niece was a bit below Graham's typical dating limit of mid-twenty-somethings. But she still hoped she and her niece didn't catch up to them on the green.

Vivian was waiting for her longtime boyfriend to pop the big question, but Graham had that certain something not many men cultivated. She had no doubt he was capable of using it to override any female's good intentions.

"You're the best ever, Aunt Doris."

"When your mother complains that I'm spoiling you, tell her it's my thank you for playing with me today. Your game is getting better."

"I know. Last time I only made ten divots instead of fifteen. I'm going to try to not do more than eight today."

Doris rolled her top lip down over her teeth and bit it to keep from laughing. If Vivian's grandparents weren't both still on the board, Vivian would have been banned from the course already. She grinned when Lloyd turned away to hide his amusement and got busy looking for a bag for Vivian's new skirt.

"Progress is progress, honey," Doris declared. "Ready to play?"

"Absolutely. Are we getting a caddy to carry our clubs?"

Doris laughed. "Is there a caddy working here that wouldn't distract you from our game?" Vivian's sigh of defeat deepened her laughter.

Doris reached out and squeezed Vivian's arm to show she was teasing. "Come on. You can carry your own bag for once. We'll stay for lunch afterward, and you can flirt with the waiters. I told my office I wouldn't be back until two thirty or three."

"I don't flirt," Vivian denied. "I'm just very friendly. It's not my fault men like me so well."

Doris ignored that sexist female comment and her niece's denial as she handed over her barely used credit card to a still grinning Lloyd. The card was a new thing for her, but she was finding it to be far more discreet than running a tab at the club—a tab she knew circulated to feed the gossip mill.

She might have learned to live with the stares and whispers of being a lone divorced woman, but she didn't want to intentionally create more. She'd done enough of that with dating some of the older, single male members. Luckily for her, a Harvard law degree was great for intimidation and for the money it provided her to pay her own way. Money was still the strongest character reference at the club.

"Have a nice game, ladies," Lloyd said, handing her the card receipt.

Doris and Vivian waved as they headed to her BMW convertible to get their clubs.

CHAPTER 2

HARRISON'S FIRST THOUGHT WHEN HE HEARD DORIS PEARSON'S
distinctive voice was that his luck was finally changing. Her clear
diction and modulated tones were unmistakable. She was
laughing in a relaxed, attractive way as she talked to her young,
blonde golf partner. In his opinion, Doris Pearson could read the
phone book and sound sexy.

When he turned his head in their direction, he saw his long-
legged idea of heaven was dressed in purple golf shorts and what
he was sure was a man's navy blue polo tucked inside them. Not
being overly endowed on top, Doris favored un-tailored shirts
without breast placeholders. Her practical, pointy support bras
made it possible for someone like him to guess her smallish size
which he didn't consider a downside. He'd always been more of a
leg man than a breast man, and he knew from experience breasts
like Doris's would fit nicely in his palms.

Since McCarthy had his head turned taking his shot, Harrison
fished a pair of binoculars out of his golf bag. Through them, he
watched as Doris yelled "Fore!" and bent to take her shot. The
next thing he heard was a swish of her club slicing the air. There
was a click, a connection, and her face took on a serene

expression of delight. Every time he saw that side of Doris, he wondered how the hell the soft spoken, serene looking woman ever managed to face down anyone in court.

"Don't bother going after that one, Graham. Those legs aren't unlocking until the woman gets a band on her hand. Rumor has it an unlucky candidate has recently stepped forward for the sacrifice—poor bastard."

Harrison lowered his binoculars. What the hell? Doris was nearly twice McCarthy's age. He could have been her son. "You dated Doris Pearson? When? You were still at school when she got divorced."

William sputtered in surprise before laughing. "Dated Doris Pearson? *Me?* Oh hell, no. I was talking about Vivian—Doris's niece. She can't play golf worth a shit, but none of the women in the club will play with her aunt, which is why she has to. Doris Pearson is no Babe Zacharias, mind you, but she's the closest thing Falls Church has to a pro. My mother says the club women don't like Doris because she chose her job over her husband. My guess is she's an ice cube. Women never seem to get the real reason men go elsewhere."

Harrison snorted and shook his head. "I don't believe any of the rumors about Doris. Club women are petty because they have nothing better to do with their time than gossip. Doris and Avery were married for over twenty years before he left her for someone Vivian's age. Don't you think Doris is well rid of the cheating bastard? I, for one, admire how she's handling her life without him."

"Yo, Reverend Hypocrite—you're preaching to the wrong choir here." William snorted and then laughed. "I'm not Doris, so don't waste your *I'm-really-a-good-guy* speech on me. You platonically date women Vivian's age all the time, but then go sleep with divorced women because they put out. Then you walk merrily away from both without a backward glance."

"It's not exactly like that," Harrison denied. And it hadn't crossed his mind that people like William McCarthy were reading such motives into his behavior.

"Please. Stop with the denial. You don't have to explain yourself to me. Besides—you could probably get Doris between the sheets, but for what purpose? She's never going to be your perfect wife. It might be worth a little something to be able to imitate that killer golf swing of hers, but that's all the good she can do a man in the long-term. She only dates older guys so you can tell she knows her place in the food chain."

Harrison had no comment to that horrible observation, mostly because the criticism about his dating habits had hit a new nerve. In all honesty, he was stalking Doris the same as he had other older women he'd hooked up with over the years.

Guilt landed squarely on his shoulders and made him hang his head for a moment. He certainly couldn't continue checking Doris out with William McCarthy critiquing his reasons. No telling what the boy would say to his parents—two of the biggest gossips at the club.

Harrison sighed quietly as they picked up their golf bags and headed to the next hole.

He needed to be more discreet in his pursuit of Doris. Unfortunately, discreet was not his style.

"THOSE PURPLE SHORTS make your long legs look really great, but you need a woman's blouse to make them look better. Why do you always wear men's shirts to play golf, Aunt Doris? Mama says that's what's holding you back. If you got a better haircut— something more modern—I bet you'd get all the dates you could ever want. It's so funny that Mama is blonde and your hair is so… brownish. How do you suppose that happened?"

The urge was strong to inform her niece that her mother's secret was bleach and blonde hair dye. Instead of venting her frustration, Doris turned her head away and settled for rolling her eyes.

In Vivian's world, a woman's focus should always be on maintaining her appearance. How could she protest that worldview when her own sister had passed that lovely vanity along to her daughter?

Doris knew lecturing her niece about the value of education was a waste of time and breath. Vivian's primary life goal was snagging a MRS Degree before her college years ended. Next time the girl came home from school, Doris expected it would be with both a cum laude diploma in her hand and a diamond ring on her finger.

A jagged breath left her mouth and she hoped her following sigh of resignation would be politely ignored by her niece. "Thank you for caring about how I look, Viv, but there's no need to concern yourself. I already have all the dates I want."

"How can that be true? Mama said you haven't dated much since your divorce."

Doris shrugged because she couldn't deny it. "At the moment, the number of dates I want is zero, honey. But if I ever feel the need for a makeover, I'll be sure and let you and your pretty blonde mama know. For the record though—I am never dying my hair. I simply don't want to, so never ask me."

"Okay," Vivian said, sighing as she looked down. "It's not like brown isn't a good hair color. It's just so... *serious.*"

"Yes, it is. That's why it suits me. I'm a serious person," Doris said as she took her stance, checked her grip, and pulled back to gauge the swing.

She was five feet ten in her golf shoes and had to use men's clubs instead of women's. The ones she had were a gently used set that had once belonged to her golf trainer's husband. Everyone in her life knew her clubs were her favorite possession.

She didn't care what people thought about her dating life or how they judged the way she dressed to please herself. Her weekly golf game was her only break from her stressful job. Out here on the green, it was just her, the ball, and a sweet, breezy challenge that didn't have anyone's life or livelihood hanging in the balance.

"What do you think of Harrison Graham, Aunt Doris?" Vivian asked.

Doris chopped her shot when she took it. She looked at the girl and snarled. "No talking until after I finish. We're not counting that one. Hand me another ball and be quiet for a full minute until I'm done swinging."

"Sorry… yes, I know. Sorry," Vivian said quickly, fishing another white ball out of her bag. "Here. I forgot for a moment. Take your shot again. I'll be quiet until you're done."

Doris lined up a second time, yelled "Fore!" and smoothly chucked the ball into the wind, which carried it within a foot of the hole. She sighed and slid her favorite driver back into the bag. She turned to her niece as she shouldered her clubs to walk.

"Thank you. Now… tell me you're not interested in Harrison Graham. The man is not a kid like Freddie. Harrison is over thirty, handsome as hell, and probably used to women putting out every time he pays for dinner. His kind is not for you, little girl. Hell, Freddie is barely for you."

Vivian giggled as they walked. *For me?* Oh no, Aunt Doris. I'm not planning to fool around with any old guys and mess things up. I'm marrying Freddie, and he's going to be my first. Mama says Freddie's family is loaded. She thinks I might even get my own house for a wedding present. Freddie will probably work in his uncle's agency as an accountant. We've nearly got our life together all worked out."

"Really? And just what do you plan to do with your own life while Freddie's working for a living?" Doris asked.

"I'll be his wife and have his babies, of course. That's why I majored in art. All those design classes will help me decorate our new house and dress our kids in a way Freddie's mom will approve of for sure. I read a lot of articles about being a good wife, and they all say it's very important for your husband's mother to approve of you."

Doris wanted to roll her eyes to the heavens, argue about sexist propaganda, and then shake some sense into the girl. But who was she to lecture on what made a good family? She'd been a married since her college days and yet had no family to show for her twenty plus years with Avery Vincent. That kind of biological success had only come to one of them.

Her ex-husband was finally going to be a father after all this time... just not to her child, even though medical science had found no reason she had never become a mother. None of Avery's other women over the years had conceived, though—and she knew they hadn't because she'd had them thoroughly investigated —yet Avery had somehow knocked up his much younger secretary in a very short period of time. The girl's extreme fertility was without question, but the unplanned pregnancy proved without further debate that the problem of never conceiving was hers.

The only good thing coming out of the sordid situation was that the woman's visible condition of being with child turned into an infidelity tipping point. The woman's pregnancy had forced her to rethink the logical, but not loving reasons, that had kept her legally bound to her habitually cheating husband. In the end, it was Avery's unborn child that drove her swift action of dissolving their relationship. She didn't need Avery or his money, but his child's mother was only a secretary. Celeste came from a wealthy family, but would need Avery's financial help for the next twenty or so years.

The unexpected bonus of her decision to finally end her unhealthy relationship was that divorcing Avery had brought her immense relief. Her marriage had been nothing but a social ruse for years—one she hadn't bothered to change because it had been better for her unusual career to be married. Most people liked the illusion that the attorney they hired was a more stable individual than they were.

Clients also liked the illusion that their female lawyer knew the intricacies of a marital relationship. She certainly *knew* a lot of intricacies. She just wasn't very good at applying them to herself.

"Do you think Freddie will be a good husband to me, Aunt Doris?"

"I don't know him well enough to answer that, Viv. What do you think?" Doris demanded softly.

Then she listened to her niece sighing in concern.

"I see our children when I look in his eyes. Do you think I'm being naïve?"

Doris sighed too. "Yes, but that's what being in love is supposed to be like. Every couple should start out starry-eyed and full of hope. Otherwise, why bother?"

During the first decade of her marriage, she had been sporadically optimistic. She'd read and sought counseling for anything Avery pointed out as a flaw. She'd traveled to Europe and hired experienced gentlemen to teach her things with a patience her husband lacked with her. Nothing she'd tried had worked, of course, but for a good many years she did keep trying back then.

The problem was her husband wanted her to be a kind of woman she wasn't ever meant to be in bed. Avery seemed relieved to stop pretending and hadn't complained a bit when she'd moved into a separate bedroom to make their separation official.

Her husband in name only hadn't shared her bed at all in the second decade they'd stayed together. She'd stayed his legal wife and frequently traveled to find fulfillment. Avery, on the other hand, had moved like a bee going from flower to flower… and he'd done so publicly.

If she'd loved Avery during that second decade, their situation would likely have destroyed her. God knew she'd handled plenty of divorces where the women never recovered from the shock of finding themselves unexpectedly alone and without income.

No one but her sister ever mentioned Avery's cheating to her. But she knew it gave the gossip committee at the country club something juicy to talk about behind her back. She was a fallen woman in their eyes just because she couldn't keep Avery happy at home.

Since her divorce, she'd dated a few men to keep the speculation headed in the direction she wanted it to go. Lately, she'd stopped trying to show the Falls Church community that she didn't care what her ex-husband did with his life.

Avery wasn't around the club to see her weak conquests among the older single men anyway. The membership had gone to her in the divorce because of her parents and because she owned quite a bit of its stock. She'd always had the real money in her marriage.

And truthfully, she was fine with being single. More than fine with it actually.

The problem was that no one would let her be okay with her reality. She often wondered what they would think if she told them what a miserable job both she and Avery had done in faking it.

"Aunt Doris? Aren't we supposed to tee up behind the line back here?"

Doris turned back and nodded. Her mind was not on her game today. Wasn't she done with regretting? She needed to be done.

Sighing, she walked back and set her stand so her golf bag would stay upright. Pulling out the perfect iron, she propped it over a shoulder. She listened to her niece clear her throat.

"Did I upset you, Aunt Doris? You never answered my question."

"No, darling. Which question?" Doris asked dully.

Vivian's optimism made her feel grumpy and old. Holy hell, though, she was tired of talking to women who forever found fault with everything she was, thought, and did. That group included her friends, her sister, and every man she'd ever had personal contact with. Sometimes she didn't think there was truly a compassionate soul left alive on the planet.

"I asked… what do you think of Harrison Graham? He was checking you out earlier."

Doris chuckled at her niece's statement, lining up for her shot. "I guarantee you the man was not checking me out. He was looking at you, Viv. All men look at you."

"No. Not him," Vivian said firmly. "When I walked to my bag, his binoculars stayed pointed in your direction. And they were tilted down at your legs."

"His binoculars were probably pointed at the ball. Maybe he's trying to pick up some tips," Doris suggested, finding Harrison Graham's spying highly amusing.

"Maybe," Vivian agreed. "Babe Zacharias did train you."

"Yes, but she wasn't the famous Babe Zacharias then," Doris replied. "She was still Babe Didrickson but just as wonderful on the green. Her golf camp was the absolute best two weeks of my life."

"You always say that, but I don't believe you. Was that golf vacation really better than your wedding and honeymoon?" Vivian demanded.

Doris rolled her eyes, but she wasn't going to lie to the girl.

"God, yes. Avery was my first lover and yet expected me on my wedding night to be like the other loose girls he'd slept with. It was a horrible first sex experience. I slept on the couch afterward and left him the next morning to go back home. The only reason Avery came after me was because his parents made him. The only reason I went back was because your grandparents talked me into it. I might have found a good man, eventually, if I'd stuck to my guns and kept looking."

Doris took the shot. It clipped the edge and the ball flew to the right, landing a good five or six feet from the hole. It made her angry that thinking of Avery in bed could affect her after all this time. How much longer was that going to go on? She'd done a lot to shed those experiences.

"Damn it. My game is completely off today, Viv," she complained aloud, even though she knew her golf game was of no interest to her niece.

"You made up with Uncle Avery, though—I mean, you stayed with him for over twenty years, so you obviously made up and fixed things back then. That's how it's supposed to work, right?" Vivian asked quietly.

Doris shook her head and frowned. "Not really, but I suppose I should be glad the illusion was believable. The truth is that we barely made up and Avery's patience with me ran out completely by the end of our first decade. We hid our problems from everyone—maybe even ourselves. Avery always claimed it was my fault we never conceived. Now instead of being considered a cheating jackass, he's seen as a good guy because he agreed to our divorce so he could marry the future mother of his love child."

She turned to see Vivian chewing her lip over her diatribe. Doris barely fought back the sigh. Her honesty was too much for the girl, but oh how she wished someone had warned her about the pitfalls of sharing your body with the wrong sort of man.

"Look—your mama married for love and your daddy still adores her. That's what marriage is supposed to be like, Viv. I picked a husband with more flaws than any woman should have to deal with in a marriage. Freddie absolutely adores you. Don't let my jaded, divorced woman attitude color your expectations of your relationship. Your opinion is the only one that matters."

"Thank you, Aunt Doris. I'm glad you like Freddie. He's perfect for me."

Doris watched the girl line up her shot and knock a crater in the ground as her ball flew in an upward arc. Since it landed closer to the hole than hers had, she couldn't say a damn word in complaint about how Vivian got it there.

Together they worked to press the turf back into place. It was like golf ballet with all the toe pointing and pressing down to convince the divot to root back into the soil. They shouldered their bags afterward and started off again.

"Mama thinks you should date younger men. I think Harrison is perfect for her idea because he's over thirty and that's old too. Mama said it would be like you getting a do-over. She said if Avery could date women half his age, then you should be allowed to date younger men. I think she's secretly hoping you will."

Doris laughed. "Well, your mother sure hasn't said anything like that to me. All I get is pity. Every time I visit, she cries as if someone died. The divorce has actually improved my situation, not made it worse. I wish I could convince her of that."

Vivian shrugged. "Daddy told her to let you live your life your way. Mama calls Avery bad names when Daddy isn't around. I think she means well with her sympathy but is just worried what you'd say if she said the mean stuff out loud to you."

Doris put her arm around her niece and hugged. Vivian was a peacemaker all around. She hoped Freddie was as good as he seemed. The last thing she wanted was to be handling another divorce in their family, so she was going to write up a marriage contract for her niece. It had taken both she and Ruth to convince the young girl of the wisdom behind it. No woman with an inheritance should ever give that up to her spouse.

"You know what I'd say to your mother? I'd tell her I don't need to be married. It's the 1960s and women can do anything they want now. Thanks for telling me all that, honey. I'll remember it next time I come to see you all."

Vivian nodded and smiled. "Okay. So back to Harrison Graham... on a scale of one to ten, how handsome do you find him. Please just tell me that much. Then I swear I'll let it go."

Doris snorted. "You have a one track mind, girl. Okay—I will admit Harrison Graham is a resounding ten. I even like those stupid Buddy Holly glasses he sometimes wears, and I like that he's a little taller than me. If the man is even half as smart as people say he is, I'd probably enjoy talking to him. If he were a decade older, I'd definitely go out to dinner. Satisfied now, Ms. Romantic?"

"Oh yes," Vivian sang. "I love you and just wanted to know you hadn't given up. I'm sure there's still time to meet someone new. You look really good for a woman your age."

"Thank you, Vivian. Coming from a happily engaged woman who looks like you do, that's a huge compliment."

As they made their way around the rest of the course, Doris laughed at the idea of her and young Graham. It was nice to know her niece thought she looked good enough for someone as handsome as Harrison was. She could afford to be amused about it all she wanted because it was never going to happen.

CHAPTER 3

Vivian sang along to the ambient music as they waited for their lunch. Doris thought it would be a miracle if the waiter managed to get it in front of them without spilling it on her niece.

She looked across the way just as Harrison entered the dining room. He was alone, and his gaze went to hers immediately, as if he'd felt her staring at him.

"Oh good Lord. I can't believe I got caught looking. Chin up, Vivian. We're getting company," Doris ordered.

"Yes, ma'am. Just putting my lipstick away," Vivian whispered before turning politely.

"Good afternoon, ladies. Did you enjoy the course this morning?" Harrison asked.

The man smiled at her and then at Vivian. Caught with having to offer social pleasantries, Doris plastered her work smile on her mouth.

"It was lovely weather. There was barely a breeze. I noticed you and William McCarthy ahead of us. You two were moving along at a good pace."

Harrison nodded. "Yes, we were. William plays a good game. He had an appointment so now I find myself alone for lunch."

Vivian smiled. "That's terrible. No one should eat alone. Would you like to join us? We've ordered, but I'm sure they could get to you quickly. The waiter is very nice."

Doris's mouth tilted at one corner. The girl was not subtle. She nodded in Vivian's direction. "Harrison, this is my niece, Vivian Waterson. She's been away at college for several years. I don't believe you've met her."

Vivian lifted her hand to him and Harrison nodded as he shook it. "I remember the announcement here about her cotillion, but that would have been several years ago. It's a pleasure to meet the grown-up version of you, Miss Waterson."

"Please... call me Vivian."

Doris fought not to roll her eyes at Vivian's gushing demand.

"My pleasure," Harrison replied, gently letting go of the younger woman's hand. He turned immediately back to Doris, conveying who he was most interested in by the action. "I'd love to join you, but I don't want to intrude on your girl time."

While he waited for the stalwart Doris to answer, Harrison grinned as annoyance flashed through her gaze. The woman didn't want him to eat with them, but he knew she'd also not want to create a scene by refusing outright. Doris's internal war with her manners barely showed on her serene face, but standing this close her irritated vibe practically reached out and smacked him. If the woman was frigid in bed, he'd eat his shoes.

"Don't be silly." Doris said as she pointed to a seat. Etiquette dictated she be gracious, but damn the man for looking so happy about it. "Please join us, Harrison. We've barely started."

"Thank you, then. I'd love to eat with you." Harrison nodded, suddenly nervous about winning the concession, and worse... he didn't know why. Normally he'd be thrilled with such a social victory.

Doris Pearson—with her sexy legs, sultry voice, and rock-solid poise—frightened him a little. Whether or not he ended up in her bed, he wanted to figure it out why she had that kind of effect on him, just to make sure it never happened again.

Pulling out the chair, he positioned it closer to Doris than her niece before sitting in it. Body language had a way of making things clear without the need for lots of words. He pretended not to notice the teasing twinkle in Vivian's gaze as it flew to her irritated, yet polite aunt's. He suspected he'd been caught looking at Doris on the course, and that the girl had mentioned it already.

Harrison lifted his head and flashed his best smile, liking it when Doris leaned back in her chair as far as she could to get away from him. He was pleased to think that the intimidation thing might be mutual.

He quickly decided that he'd better just confess so she wouldn't think he was sneaky. "I was watching your swing earlier. I hope you don't mind. You looked like a real professional out there on the course."

Doris wondered how long she could be stiffly polite without inventing a sudden illness and dashing to the ladies room. Avoiding social confrontation was not her style, but she'd seen Vivian and her sister feigning problems often enough to know how to do it. Wanting to so badly was the only reason she wouldn't give in to the urge to flee Harrison's company. Vivian had made her hyper conscious of Harrison Graham's potential interest in her. Acting nervous around him simply wouldn't do.

"Thank you," she said stiffly. "I sincerely love the game. I only play for fun these days, but I do my best. Vivian and I don't keep score. I only keep mine mentally in my head so I know when I'm falling off my stride."

"Did you always just play for fun? I would find that surprising after what I saw." Harrison chuckled at her irritation over his compliment. He also wondered what Doris would think if he told her the mental math she did turned him on as much as her fine—very fine—legs.

Vivian spoke, surprising them both with the interruption.

"Aunt Doris doesn't brag about it, but she was trained by Babe Zacharias. She even played the semi-pro women's circuit for years in her late 20s and early 30s, but gave it up when she made partner in her law firm. Mama said Aunt Doris could have been every bit as good as Babe if she'd just stayed with it."

Doris barely stifled her snort. What her sister had actually said was that she should play golf for fun as a sexy wife instead of giving it up to work as a successful, unsexy lawyer. Then she would have had more time for cooking dinner and dressing to appeal to her routinely unfaithful husband. Since Doris had been contemplating her eventual divorce even back then, that choice would have been a foolish one.

"Vivian... stop. I'm sure Harrison isn't interested in such old news."

Harrison smiled at the girl's praise and ignored Doris's false modesty. "From what I saw out there, I can certainly agree with that evaluation of your aunt's skills. Maybe she and I can play a game sometime and your talented aunt can give me some pointers."

Harrison smiled wider when Vivian beamed at his suggestion. He expected any minute to be stabbed with the fork Doris was suddenly gripping like a weapon, but it would be worth it just to see her crack. Fascinated, he watched as Doris tried to formulate a polite refusal, but her exuberant niece took that issue out of her aunt's polite hands as well by speaking for her. He was sure the cute little blonde was one of the few people who ever lived after doing so.

"Aunt Doris would love to help you. Wouldn't you, Aunt Doris? She needs someone who can give her a better game than me. No one here at this club is in her league, but you looked like you were winning out there."

Harrison laughed at having been stalked back. Too bad it had been by the wrong woman. He turned to the right one and caught her glaring before she carefully erased her reaction from her expression. In her hesitation, he saw his opening. This was going to be even easier than he'd dreamed. He looked at the younger woman, then slyly at Doris.

"I couldn't ask her to do that, Vivian. The club doesn't like mixed gender games. They don't forbid them, but I wouldn't want to cause your aunt any embarrassment here at the club. I'm sure she's had enough of that in her life."

Doris didn't blink as she stared into Harrison's amused gaze. It was the look she gave jurors to make sure she had their attention before speaking. He was offering her a total out, yet it also sounded like he'd just issued a challenge. How did they get involved in this verbal war in less than ten minutes? Seeing Harrison's handsome head made you forget there was a brain inside it... until he got shrewd with you.

The waiter arrived and took Harrison's attention from her briefly. Across the table, Vivian was practically holding her breath as she stared at her.

Damn. Damn. Damn.

Whatever she answered, it was going straight back to her sister via her man-crazy niece. Within two days, her parents would probably know all about it too. Stall? Yes, that might work. She just needed to stall until she could find a way to turn the man's request down politely.

"At my age, I'm not worried much about what people say anymore," Doris began, "but my court schedule is going to be extremely busy for the next two weeks. I'd have to check my calendar for times we could possibly play. Can I get back to you?"

Harrison wanted to clap at being so smoothly out-maneuvered, but he smiled and nodded instead. "Of course. I'm just happy you're even considering it."

"Yay!"

They both turned sharp gazes when Vivian squealed before calming herself. Doris glared. Harrison chose to smile at the girl and wink.

Vivian cleared her throat as her face turned pink. "I'm sorry. I'm starved and just excited about the food coming. Our waiter stuck his head out of the kitchen door and signaled it would be five more minutes."

Harrison fought not to laugh at the girl's polite lie. Doris's irritation was equally noticeable and much more amusing. They all knew Vivian's explanation was a cover for her slip, but such a thing could not be called out at a polite lunch in front of other club members.

Harrison grinned when he realized how interested he was in this drama. He would have given a lot to have heard their discussion about him out on the green. Maybe one day he'd get lucky enough to find out what had been said.

Harrison cleared his throat to signal he was changing the subject. "I read this morning that RCA stock took another downturn. Glad I sold my shares before that happened."

Some of Doris's irritation seeped away as she turned to Harrison. She was grateful he had the good grace to overlook Vivian's outburst. "I read that this morning too. I sold my RCA stock last month and shifted my portfolio to focus on technology companies. That's the next big wave I think. I heard a rumor about a new company based off Dartmouth BASIC coming soon. It's going to be focused on building processors for computers. I want to be liquid enough to invest when that happens in a couple years. I have a very good feeling about it."

Harrison nodded, nearly mute with admiration. He had to clear his throat to respond. "We have a lot in common, Ms. Pearson. Do you do your own investment research?"

Doris shrugged, trying not to be impressed with how Harrison had addressed her. She had kept her maiden name for professional use and flatly refused to call herself Mrs. Avery Vincent anywhere that didn't demand it. While she didn't consider herself a feminist, the label had been attached to her for that decision. Women in this club were likely convinced of her leanings now that she was divorced.

She pulled out of her thoughts to see Harrison patiently waiting for her to answer. "I do some research, but I also have a great financial guy who points me in the right direction. Larry thinks the real money is going to be in electronic pieces and parts over the next decade because soon everyone will have a computer in their home."

Harrison nodded again. "I agree with him. It's only a matter of time. People usually laugh when I say it, though. I envy you your financial confidante."

When Vivian giggled, Doris noticed they both turned to her at the same time.

"You two are so funny. What would a family do with a computer? Men don't need to work at home. They need to *relax* at home," Vivian declared, dismissing the idea with a wave of her beautifully manicured nails. "I'm not trying to be old-fashioned, just practical."

Doris snorted and shook her head. She'd never been that young and naïve. She was absolutely sure of it. Favoring her niece with a challenging gaze, she tightened her tone as she spoke. "I would get a computer just to do my investment research in the privacy of my own home."

"Yes," Harrison agreed. "Not to mention using it to keep an inventory of all your possessions. A person could nearly operate an entire business out of their garage if they had programs to help with the accounting and billing."

"Damn—that's a terrifically smart idea, Harrison. You should write it all out and try to find someone to do the work. You could maybe even get a patent on it."

"Aunt Doris… shh. You swore in the dining room. You don't want to have to pay the obscenity fine again."

Caught by surprise—because she'd been enjoying the conversation—Doris narrowed her gaze as she glared at her niece.

"Don't shush me, Vivian. We've had this talk. I believe in freedom of speech, and I did not pay that fine. Your mother paid that fine because your grandmother kept complaining about our social duty to set a moral example. However, morality is not the same as pompous religiosity. I will speak however I like wherever I like. It's a free country, even for women who belong to this damn, uptight club."

Vivian wiggled in her chair. "Please lower your voice. I didn't mean to offend you, Aunt Doris. Our family might be used to your speech habits, but you're probably embarrassing Harrison."

Doris turned and looked at the smiling man. Harrison Graham didn't seem the type to get embarrassed about anything. Hell, he'd practically invited himself to lunch with them. But she'd play the stupid game for Vivian's sake. The juicier gossip of her apology might keep nearby eavesdroppers from reporting her.

"I'm sorry for my slip, Mr. Graham. Am I embarrassing you with my intense language?"

Harrison pursed his lips, fighting the grin for all he was worth. He squirmed, trying to discreetly shift what was happening in his lap to a more comfortable position.

"Quite the contrary, Ms. Pearson. I find you more appealing now than ever. There's nothing more interesting than an intelligent woman who speaks her mind. Sadly, you're an endangered species in Falls Church, Virginia."

Now, Doris knew why Harrison had scored with every woman who'd ever caught his eye. Maybe he believed what he said or maybe he didn't. That particular truth didn't matter to her at the moment.

She instantly forgave him everything when Vivian turned a totally shocked gaze in his direction. He had effortlessly done in thirty seconds what she'd spent literally years trying to accomplish. He'd shown her niece a true glimpse of how different the world was from what her parents had told her.

Doris smiled at Harrison for real. "That may be the nicest

compliment I've ever had in my life. Are you just saying that because you want golf lessons?"

"No, I'm saying that because I mean it. I always mean what I say. It's a family trait. My mother was brutal in her opinions, but I don't like to think I'm quite that bad. But about the golf lessons… I am very interested. Maybe I could do something for you in return. Tit for tat, you know."

"Tit for tat?" Doris snorted as she repeated the phrase. Teasing bastard. She was short on the tit part, but her tat was just fine. "Really? Like what would you offer in return for my training services?"

Harrison bowed his head as he grinned. "I'm sure something interesting will come up—something you need help with. Whatever it is, I'll be your man for it."

Her eye-roll over his innuendo couldn't be prevented. His laughter over her reaction made her want to run away again. She lifted a finger and pointed it at his chest without touching him. It was a move she often used in closing arguments in court.

"You've made a case I can't argue against. Okay—you've got yourself a golf teacher. Call my office tomorrow. I'll have my schedule figured out by then."

"Yes, ma'am," Harrison answered, eyeing the food placed in front of him.

He'd been a starving man when he sat down at their table.

Now he was about to have a feast.

CHAPTER 4

THURSDAY MORNING WAS CRYSTAL CLEAR, ESPECIALLY AT SEVEN forty-five. Lloyd hadn't batted an eye when they'd met at the counter. Doris had talked Lloyd into letting them on the green early. She said she had to be at work by nine, but Harrison suspected Doris was just trying to stay ahead of other early birds… and under the gossip radar.

"If you'd waited, I would have put the green fees on my credit card," she said.

Today, Doris was wearing a pair of long tan shorts that practically hid her knees and what Harrison was sure was a man's v-neck golf sweater over a man's polo shirt. He was trying to figure out if her cross-dressing was a fashion choice or indicated something deeper about her character he needed to heed as a warning. Wanting badly to see the body beneath the butt ugly outfit was still driving him crazy, so his plan wasn't to overthink it.

Harrison raised an eyebrow at the woman carrying a set of professional men's clubs that were probably heavier than his. Was that another sign his interest in her was a bad idea? Maybe.

Once again the sign in his pants when she smiled at the sunshine and breeze was a larger influence.

"Why would you pay? Playing with you was my idea. The least I can do is pay green fees, Ms. Rich Attorney," he joked.

Doris chuckled. "Oh, you'll pay all right. Your tab for today's game with our names on it will get circulated to prove our game is not merely gossip, but the gospel truth."

Harrison chuckled along with her because Doris was right. "Point made. Do you care that's going to be the case? I don't." He wanted to be linked to her. He just wasn't sure why yet. But he sure as hell wasn't ever wearing his v-necked sweater when they played. They'd look like twins.

Doris shook her head and laughed. "After the grist mill Avery put me through, I doubt playing golf with even a notorious younger man like you can make matters worse. I would appreciate it, though, if you'd choose your next bed partner outside the club. My female reputation is already in the toilet here. I don't really care, but my parents do, and they're still on the board."

Harrison frowned. "I would never embarrass you, at least not on purpose. I watched what my mother went through with my father. I always try to be discreet."

"Yes, I'm sure you try, but you don't often succeed. No one does around here, but don't worry, Harrison. It's not like it's your fault. It's this small town and the small minds of those who control the wealth in it."

"You and I control some of that wealth," Harrison said sharply, wondering why he was bothered by her low opinion of his dating life. He'd never made any woman any promises. He sure as hell hadn't married any to gain anything. "You and I are not all that small-minded. Don't we count?"

"Two is too small a number to matter. I could prove your worst catty female fears about this place are a stark reality if I chose to do so. Want me to list the women you've slept with in the last three months?" Doris asked, parking her bag on its prop stand. "And I think we should make a pact not to discuss our checkered pasts on the green after today. It's too distracting. We'll talk through it for eighteen holes, then no more. Agreed?"

Harrison frowned and wondered why Doris's composure irked him so badly. He wasn't a client of hers, and she wasn't a business contract to him. Maybe he was irritated because Doris seemed clueless about his real interest in her. He would have thought the woman was smarter than that. If she was, she gave no sign of it to him.

"The last time I slept with a woman affiliated with this club was over nine months ago. The actual last time I slept with any woman was over four. She was a newly divorced cocktail waitress from Arlington who I met in a hotel in DC. We'd both had two too many. Nature took its course. I don't even remember her name. I doubt she remembers mine. Those experiences are never all that great."

Doris laughed at the detailed confession. "I wasn't asking for a report. Save your bragging for your man friends. If it doesn't affect your golf swing, what you do is not important to me." She pointed. "Tee off first. Let me see your form. I need to know what you can do."

Harrison fetched one of his balls and pulled his most trusted driver from his bag. He shoved a tee in the ground and set his ball on it. "Don't stare at my ass, Doris. If you do, you might end up being the reason I have to change my story. I've heard lots of reports about how cute it is."

The woman snickered as he lined up his shot. He was nervous as hell with Doris watching him, and irritated as hell because she looked everywhere *but* at his ass. Not even a side glance was directed at his hips. Instead, she focused on his hands and feet.

The woman had the unique ability to tune him out seemingly whenever she wanted. That wasn't a pleasant trait—or at least not one he was used to in women.

His driver glanced off one side of the ball and sent his shot flying toward the woods. Damn it. It was quite possibly the worst he'd ever done playing a partner. He got lucky, though, and the ball curved back at the last minute rolling about eight feet away from the hole. Barely restraining himself from rubbing his forehead in relief, he realized he'd still make under par —maybe.

"Tell me you're not of those who rely on luck," she demanded. "Your cute ass won't get you by forever, Harrison."

"Obviously, you haven't played golf with a male partner in a while. If you were William McCarthy, I'd tell you where to shove that remark."

When Doris laughed at his rebuttal, Harrison raised his hands. "I know it was bad, but I kept it on the green, didn't I? How am I supposed to play well with you staring at me so hard?"

"Lots of practice," Doris replied. She pulled her favorite driver and a ball from the bag. Still smiling, she passed by a nearly glaring Harrison and set up for her shot.

Grinning for all she was worth, Doris drew back and sent a smooth sailing hit flying toward its goal. If it had rolled just a little more, she would have aced the shot. Still… landing a few inches from the cup was astoundingly better than she usually hit on the par three, number one hole slanted toward the trees.

Harrison grumbled and harrumphed the whole time she was taking her shot, so she was especially proud of herself for managing to ignore him.

She turned to the man now frowning at her. "In a couple weeks, you'll be making shots like this. Next hole, I'll help you line yourself up better."

Harrison stared for a full minute without answering. Crude sexual innuendo was on the tip of his tongue. He wanted to tell Doris that he never missed sinking a perfect shot when it really counted. But the woman was smiling, fully expecting something like that to tumble from his lips, and he didn't want to give her the satisfaction. It was going to be a long eighteen, though, if he couldn't develop a better tolerance for her wit.

"Fine," Harrison declared finally. "I'm an outstanding student, Ms. Pearson. When we get down to real business, I will make sure you don't have any complaints about my performance."

Doris grinned as she returned her club to the bag and hefted it over a shoulder. "Your performance history speaks for itself. I'm sure it has to be true because I've heard it from my sister, who is a gossip of the highest caliber around here."

Faced with her nearly unshakeable composure, Harrison felt like a high school geek trying to talk his way into a cheerleader's pants. He'd never been one of those, or at least had never seen himself as one, but he'd always been a keen observer of those who were willing to risk crashing and burning in pursuit of a goal.

EIGHT HOLES LATER, they had run out of time. Ironically, Doris's job demands ended up being a save for him. He didn't know how much more he could take without revealing the truth of what he was experiencing.

Doris might not have stared at his ass, but for the last hour the woman had managed to put her hands on nearly every inch of his ass's real estate, as well as just about everything else below his belt. She'd spread his legs with one of hers, tilted his hips any way she'd wanted, and had even stabilized his entire body by leaning her entire body against him as he took the absolute best golf swing of his entire life.

Walking from hole to hole with her had been torturous. Three times he'd faked a way to discreetly adjust his expanding interest. Doris in her man's sweater and man's shirt had gone on instructing as if she had no idea she stiffened him with her every touch.

They played the number nine hole in complete silence. He'd

never known a woman who could go that long without talking. Since he normally lacked the ability to keep quiet himself, he'd never expected it of anyone he'd dated. They were walking the golf cart path back to the club and were halfway there before Doris spoke again.

"I've enjoyed our game, Harrison. I think I'm free next Tuesday morning if you want to do this again."

Harrison nodded at the first couple of people who gawked at their passing. When the gawking number grew to being everyone they passed, he decided ignoring them was the better strategy. Doris talked politely as if unaware. She was keeping pace with his stride better than most men his height did. And she wasn't a bit winded carrying those enormous clubs of hers.

It wasn't that being with Doris was outright emasculating. He just didn't know his place. Her actions and intelligent conversation kept pointing out how his hard-won knowledge about women didn't really apply to her.

He stopped alongside her car when she set down her bag to unlock the trunk. Wordlessly, Harrison hefted up her clubs for her and laid the bag in the tidy area she revealed. He was a neatnik too, but for some reason it bothered him to discover Doris was. Her organized car trunk meant she liked to control all aspects of her life, and he was desperately seeking some crack in that self-confident exterior she presented to the world.

Hell's bells, the woman had him turning cartwheels and doing handstands, and he still couldn't figure her out.

"Coming to the charity dance Friday night?" he asked.

Doris closed the trunk with a firm click. "I donate, but usually don't attend those functions. A divorced woman coming alone to something on a Friday night looks rather pathetic, don't you think?"

Harrison narrowed his gaze. "Why? I come alone all the time. Men never think that way about such things. It surprises me you do, but I understand. Everyone has a limit to their social bravery."

The challenge was now issued. He'd have to show up himself just on the off chance Doris would. He didn't come to those functions either, but it probably wasn't something she'd easily believe about him.

Doris took in a deep breath and looked back toward the green. He could nearly see her brain working it out. People were already talking. If Doris showed up and danced with five or six men, that might go a long way to keeping people guessing about her personal business. Harrison watched the decision show first in the direct gaze she brought back to him. He wasn't surprised to see her finally nod.

"Maybe you're right, Harrison. I never looked at it that way. If I have time, I might come by. I used to love to dance. Avery wasn't much for it. Plus, it might be fun to dress up for a night."

Harrison shrugged, playing it as cool as he could, but a grin gave him away. "Save me one in case I show up. I have to check and see if I have a date scheduled. Sometimes I forget."

"I fear *looking* pathetic, Mr. Graham. I didn't say I actually was. Show up and get on my dance card like all the others—unless you bring a date. If you do, stay the hell away from me. I have enough problems," Doris ordered, grinning back.

Harrison tipped an imaginary hat. "I've been chastised properly. Thanks for the golf pointers. Have a good day, Ms. Pearson."

"Same to you, Mr. Graham. Don't rob any old ladies out of their fortunes. I've heard you're ruthless out of bed as well."

"I am, but I only do ruthless things on Mondays. Every other day of the week I rescue widows and orphans," Harrison teased, waving good-bye.

CHAPTER 5

Doris had gone through every dress in her closet before settling on a knee-length green chiffon dress with an attached short train that stopped at the hem. Judging from the absence of a theme and decorations, the outfit was probably too elegant for this sort of dance, but none of the others had seemed right either. Her mother and sister would have killed her if she'd come in one of her lawyer suits.

Sighing, Doris ran her hand down the green chiffon and promised herself to buy some party clothes in the next couple of weeks.

"You haven't worn that dress since the Anderson wedding. It looks as great on you now as it ever did."

Doris turned, frowned, and put a hand on her hip. "Why are you here, Avery? You're not a member any longer. Don't make me run home and get our divorce decree to prove it."

She fumed as Avery shrugged his shoulders inside an impeccable suit. He'd lost some weight and stepped up his grooming. It was typical divorced man behavior, but she didn't care as much when she saw a client do it. Seeing such things in her cheating ex-husband made her itch to physically remove the grin from his face.

"Cool your jets, Counselor. I was a member when I made a donation to the charity being supported tonight. I didn't break any club commandments coming here."

Doris narrowed her eyes and glared. "I think that depends on whether we're speaking figuratively or not. Where is your new bride, Avery? Kick the poor woman to the curb already?"

"Something like that," Avery agreed. "Ask me again next week. I may have some real news then."

Doris shook her head. "Are you really that cold-hearted? You can't dump a woman who's having your child."

"You can if she's involved with someone else," Avery declared. "I wish I'd never left you."

Doris snorted. "You didn't. I kicked you out. It was time."

Avery laughed. "I miss you, Doris. I miss you every day. You're the only person I could never bullshit. If I end my current relationship, will you let me come home?"

Doris shook her head. "No. Never again in this lifetime. We are over."

Two of the biggest gossips in the club appeared at her elbow. They said hello to Avery, complimented her dress, and smiled shyly. She knew what the rumor was going to be tomorrow, but there wasn't a damn thing she could do about it. Then she heard another voice.

"Hello ladies. Doris, if your dance card isn't full, may I take you for a spin?"

Doris's mouth lifted at one corner. Harrison wasn't wearing a white hat, but at least he'd come to rescue her. "I just got here, Mr. Graham. My card is completely empty. I will also confess that I came alone tonight. How about you?"

She ignored the gasps over her direct question. They were drowned out by Harrison's husky loud chuckle over her nerve.

"You're safe. My calendar was empty after all. Come on golf

partner, let's hit the floor and make showing up worth our while," Harrison said, holding out a hand.

"My pleasure. Excuse me please," Doris said to Avery and the gossip crows, smiling sweetly as she let Harrison lead her to the floor.

Once in his arms, she let out a breath. "Thanks for the rescue."

"I know what the women wanted. What the hell did Avery want?"

Doris rolled her eyes. "The self-centered jackass wanted me to take him back. I told him to do the right thing and take care of the mother of his child."

Harrison nodded in approval against her hair. His lips were level with Doris's ear in the taller shoes she wore. A slight shift of his head and he could have his mouth on hers. She was wearing a light perfume that made him want to find out where she'd dabbed it on herself.

"For someone so out of practice, you dance pretty well," Harrison whispered. He wanted to also tell her she looked beautiful, but was fearful it might set her off. Her body was tense against his. Dealing with Avery had obviously put her on edge.

Doris sighed and relaxed in Harrison's arms at his simple praise. "You dance well too," she whispered back, content to let him move her around the floor, even if all eyes were glued to them.

When the song ended, Harrison had to surrender Doris to another man asking for a dance. There were three more after that one and his patience was frayed by the time he could ask her again. She immediately leaned against his arm. His gaze fell to her feet.

"Need saving again?" he asked.

Doris laughed as he accurately guessed her problem. "My feet are killing me in these taller heels. Do you mind if we head outside for a break so I can take these shoes off for a while."

Harrison offered his arm as he nodded. Getting Doris alone?

He was all about it—any time and any way he could. "Your wish is my command."

Outdoors Doris limped as gracefully as possible to a bench, collapsing on it. Groaning softly she took off her heels and set them beside her.

Harrison stood a few feet away, hands in pockets, watching her every move. His alertness made her laugh. "I'm fine, Harrison. I just haven't played dress-up in a while."

"I'm sorry now that I goaded you into coming here. This place is…" Harrison shrugged, knowing he didn't have to say more for her to understand.

Doris laughed. "You didn't exactly goad me into coming, and I'm having a good time dancing. It's just these damn shoes. It's been twelve years since I had them on. I should have just worn my court heels."

"The shorter ones would have destroyed the beautiful symmetry of your legs in that dress. I fully appreciate the choice you made," Harrison said. "And I'm probably not the only one."

Doris rolled her eyes at his compliment, and it pissed him off. He pulled one hand from his pocket and erased two feet of the distance between them. Looking down, he watched as she lifted one foot—no small feat in the narrow skirt—and rubbed her own instep.

Acting on an urge that surprised him, Harrison squatted and took over the task. Her grateful groan echoed through him. He wanted to help her make that sound all night. A hundred ways to do so started running through his mind.

"Your feet are awfully small for a woman your height. No wonder they can't hold you up in heels."

Doris stopped groaning to stare at him so he set that foot down and picked up her other one.

"You look incredibly beautiful tonight. I wanted to tell you earlier, but I figured your ex had beat me to offering the compliment."

Doris swallowed to steady her voice. It was a trick she'd learned long ago. A judge didn't pay attention to a female attorney unwilling to speak up.

"Avery did tell me. So did every man I danced with. None have your simple sincerity, Harrison. I actually believe you when you say it."

Before he could catch himself and stifle his action, Harrison ran a hand up the back of her stocking covered leg and under the edge of her skirt to the snaps at mid-thigh. His fingers trembled slightly as he traced skin beneath the sexy garter. He rose to his knees and covered her to prevent prying eyes from seeing what he was doing.

"Careful there, Casanova. We may not be alone. I think I saw Lydia Smithfield come out here earlier," Doris whispered.

Harrison nodded. "She runs away from her parents and McCarthy every chance she gets. Maybe if she sees us, she'll know this is what happens when two people are sincerely attracted to each other. I'm tired of hiding it, Doris. Kiss me."

Her mouth opened on a gasp at his demand and his mouth covered hers, unrepentantly taking full advantage. He expected a hard push away or at least a firm hand on his shoulder to make him stop. Instead, he felt strong fingers inside his suit coat slipping around the back to urge him closer. He pulled away on principle... and because he didn't want to ruin their first kiss by making out with her in this damn place.

Doris sighed and moved her hand back to her lap. "You're right. I am attracted to you. Want to come home with me tonight?"

Harrison rose and backed away a couple feet. He couldn't have heard her right. He watched dumbfounded as Doris slipped her heels back on and stood up to look him straight in the eye.

"Well?" she demanded. "You seemed enthusiastic enough a moment ago. Does it bother you that I had the audacity to ask you first?"

Harrison absently nodded. "But I still want to say yes," he finally answered, not stupid enough to pass up the chance, no matter how shocked he was. "Do you make that offer to men often?" He wanted to call the words back immediately, but her smirk prevented the apology from escaping.

"No—I don't. I usually go to their place. That way I can leave when I want to," Doris said. She fisted one hand against her hip. "Don't worry. I've never made that offer here, not even to anyone in Falls Church. It's a bad idea to shit where you eat. Isn't that what they say?"

Harrison nodded again, not sure what to think of her gross analogy. Obviously fed up, Doris rolled her eyes and started to walk away. His hand reached out, swung her around, and his mouth was on hers again. They were both breathing hard when he could finally make himself let her go.

Reality returned slowly. When it did, his hands were on her ass, and her hands were on his. Well, okay. He could live with learning she was a bold woman. He stepped away from Doris and dug in his pocket for a pen, shocked further when Doris laughed at him.

"Stop posturing. You know where I live. I told you... no head games," she chastised.

Harrison sighed and put the pen back in his pocket. "You really don't play the polite game, do you?"

Doris laughed and the sound filled the courtyard. Everyone hiding among the arbors, fountains, and trees would have heard her. He tried to figure out if he cared. The jury in his brain was still out on the matter when she spoke again.

"No, Mr. Graham. I don't play the polite game well. I've made more exceptions than usual for you. Are you coming with me or not?"

Harrison snorted at the demand. Innuendo? Again he couldn't tell with her. "If you couldn't glean my response from our kissing, you're in denial. Lead the way, woman. I'm right behind you."

He intended to be behind her, in front of her, and everywhere else she'd let him be, all night long.

CHAPTER 6

AT DORIS'S DIRECTION, HARRISON PARKED IN THE EMPTY SECOND bay of her three car garage located just to the left of her house. A breezeway lined with jasmine covered trellises connected the two.

Doris didn't live in a mansion, but it was close to being one. Her home was a renovated old estate house with more rooms than any family could ever use, though he'd heard her great-grandparents had filled this place with their nine children.

He entered and found himself standing in her enormous kitchen. Beyond the glass doors was a paver patio, lawn furniture, and another arbor covered in more jasmine as well as multiple varieties of colorful flowers he didn't recognize.

Inside the kitchen was homey, but also modern. There was an island with bar stools, something you didn't see often. One lone place setting at the end of it revealed the owner's penchant for dining alone. But everything else spoke of hospitality and comfort. His family home—the one his father occupied—was large, but not nearly this put together.

There were distinct differences between a house and a home. He knew because he'd personally owned three houses since his mid-twenties and sold each for a tidy profit. None of them had ever held any real appeal as the place he wanted to stay forever. They had been just places he spent the night. He'd never brought any woman to any of them either. In his mind, hotels were better suited for liaisons. Paying for room service usually made up for the lack of personal ambience.

Doris said she didn't bring men home. If true, why then was he here? He was already imagining himself drinking coffee with her out on her patio. Doing so would be another first for him, but he was coming to think of such ideas as the "Doris effect" on his life.

When his surprised hostess found him, he was staring out her back door at the comfy table and chairs that looked so inviting. Doris was still wearing her pretty green dress… but now the heels were missing. Harrison found himself looking down at her for once. It was a little thing between them, those two or three inches in height, but knowing he was taller somehow helped him deal with the reverse seduction he wasn't yet comfortable with.

"Are you sure about this?" he asked.

Harrison realized it had been the exact wrong thing to say when a no longer smiling Doris left his side and walked to a long counter where a re-corked bottle of red wine sat. She pulled two glasses from a nearby rack and poured out liberal drinks for both of them. Neither of them had imbibed at the club. But he didn't blame her for needing a little liquid courage. Maybe he did too.

Leaving the bottle uncorked, Doris carried the two glasses back with her and handed one off to him. He watched as she lifted hers for a sip before she spoke.

"Author Victor Hugo said that female curiosity is a form of feminine bravery. I agree with him. Am I sure I want you here? Yes. Am I afraid? Also, yes. But I'm brave enough to indulge my feminine curiosity about you. That's really all this is. I hardly know you, but I tend to follow my instincts."

Harrison reached out and lifted her hand, the one without a wine glass in it. Her fingers trembled in his. Sometimes her honesty put him off. This was not one of those times. "Curiosity is good enough for me. Can we go outside and drink our wine? I was admiring your patio."

"Sure. I'll need my hand back to open the door, though."

Harrison chuckled at her quick reply and let go of her fingers slowly. "Okay, but I'm holding your hand again when we get outside. I like touching you."

"Okay," Doris said back, struggling to push open the door. It had a tendency to stick. She handed Harrison her glass, then shoved hard against it with her whole weight until it popped open. "There—finally. This door always sticks."

"The bottom of your door needs planed off a little," Harrison commented as they crossed the threshold.

"The door needs what?" Doris asked. Then she laughed. "I'm not very handy around the house. Sounds like you're speaking Greek."

Harrison laughed, relieved to find at least one thing in the world that Doris Pearson didn't understand as well as he did. Maybe he was more sexist than he realized. Anything was possible.

"Wood swells over time. The wood on the bottom of the door needs to be shaved off with a smoothing plane. Then it won't be so hard to open."

"Oh. Do you know how to do that?"

Harrison nodded at her question. "When you renovate houses for resale, you learn a lot of useful things. If I can't get to it in the next little bit, I'll send over a guy I know who does a good job."

"Send the guy tomorrow. I'll gladly pay him," Doris said, sipping her wine. "Avery wasn't useful that way, and when he tried, he only made problems worse. I never let him touch my house. He never sat out here anyway. The patio was my haven."

Harrison arched an eyebrow. "You let me into your haven *and* you trust me not to hurt your house. I knew you were a smart woman. So does this mean you're going with your gut about me?"

Doris sat in one of the cushioned chairs around the table. It wasn't completely dark, but the moonlight was already bouncing off the white hydrangeas that flanked the entry to the gardens. The covering over her beloved patio was her gift to herself when she made partner. Avery hadn't even said congratulations. He never asked about her work so he hadn't known until someone at the club had told him.

She looked at the handsome man she was about to take as a lover. She knew that she would have told Harrison. He might not have liked that she'd made partner either, but she had a feeling he'd have dealt with a higher earning wife more gracefully than Avery had. She'd bought her ex-husband a sports car with her first bonus to put them back on a friendly footing. Placating Avery's ego had cost her lots of money over the years. He'd cost her a lot personally too.

"Yes, I trust you not to hurt my house," Doris conceded, when she realized he was still waiting for her to reply. "I can only hope that extends to the rest of me as well."

Harrison snorted and gave her a glare over his wine. "Doll, I'm certainly not going to hurt you. In fact, I'm going to treat you so damn well you'll want to keep me."

"For a little while I think I like you… and then there's that damn bragging thing you do," Doris pointed out as she smirked. "I hate braggarts and drunks."

"You handed me the wine, so I don't want to hear anything about my drinking. And it's not bragging if it's true. I also know how to take direction. For Exhibit A, I offer my already improved golf swing as evidence. I will be outstanding in bed. What I refuse to be is a one-night stand. I know that's what you're probably offering, but I want more from you than that. I want us to at least be friends."

Doris set her wine glass down and sighed. "Shit, I'm sorry. Do I really come across so cold and exacting? I honestly don't mean to. I have no idea how I will feel about you in the morning, so it wouldn't be fair to promise anything. The truth is I used up my bold thoughts about us just deciding to ask you here. Your kiss made me too dizzy with lust to think clearly."

Harrison chuckled. "This deal is sounding better all the time to me." He put a hand on the table and turned it palm up. He watched Doris stare at his hand for a few long, tortuous moments, but she finally took it.

"I haven't held hands since high school," she complained.

"Get used to it," Harrison ordered. "I like holding hands... well, I like holding *your* hand. I don't think I've thought much about it before you."

"This doesn't exactly feel like a seduction, Harrison."

Harrison nodded, holding her gaze. "That's because it's not. This is a growing friendship... maybe a courtship. Believe me, you'll know when we get to the seduction part."

"Bragging again?" she asked.

He pulled her hand to his mouth kissing every knuckle before pressing his lips to the center of her palm. "You look beautiful in that dress, but all I really want to do is to peel it off you and see what's underneath."

"I've been ready for that since you kissed me earlier. Just say when."

He came around to her side of the table, knelt at her feet, and reached up under her dress. She didn't once try to stop him. Her legs parted for him instead, and his hands started to shake over the many possibilities crossing his mind. Somehow he still managed to get her garters unsnapped. He rolled down the high quality nylons and slid them off her exquisitely smooth, bare legs. Once he'd freed her, he stood and toed off his own shoes, and bent to peel off his socks as well. When he was finished, he held out a hand.

"Fancy a barefoot walk in the gardens, Ms. Pearson? I want to kiss you in the moonlight."

"Mr. Graham, that is the absolute best offer I've had in ages."

Doris stood on trembling legs, her bare feet registering the warm pavers. She hadn't walked barefoot in her own yard in years. Harrison led her out to where the magnolias would bloom in a month. The already succulent honeysuckle and wild roses filled her senses, but it was the man wickedly smiling at her that she was always going to remember about tonight.

~

THOUGH SHE DIDN'T QUITE KNOW how it had gotten there, her dress was now pooled at her feet. Harrison's hands seemed to be everywhere at once. His touch was tender in one place and urgent in another. When he lifted her hips against his and surged between her thighs, she'd had enough.

Her hands undid buttons, his belt, and the zipper of his fly. She reached inside and gripped him, nearing bringing both of them to their knees.

"Come inside with me," he said hoarsely. "Let's finish this in a bed."

Everything important in her life had narrowed to needing Harrison Graham inside her so she wasn't about to say no. Doris stepped out of her dress and snatched it up before he could drag her away. On the trip back to the house, she smiled and hoped she could come up with a convincing lie to explain the grass stains to her dry cleaner.

Harrison dragged her across her patio in her underwear, her white garters still dangling down her legs. Their every swing against her thighs was a reality check. Every glance he gave her made her more nervous about what was to come.

Anticipation raised goosebumps all over her as she trailed after him until he started up the stairs. Digging her heels in, she tugged back and laughed. "Nice guess, Sherlock, but I sleep down here. I turned two rooms around the corner into a ground floor master suite."

"It better have a bed because the floor is looking better and better. Take me there," Harrison ordered.

His hoarse, cranky tone made her giggle, something she rarely did. Doris was pretty sure it was the man and not the wine causing it. His flirting had distracted her from having more than one glass.

She stopped at her doorway, turned to face him, and wrapped her hand in one flapping side of his unbuttoned shirt. She put her lips to his collar bone and sniffed as she kissed him there. The man was all lean muscle under his modern clothes. She felt lucky —very, very lucky—to be sharing this moment with him.

She lifted her face and put her mouth on his as she backed into the bedroom, luring him with her kiss. Their kiss spun out, making her dizzy. That was another surprise. Every lip press caused the same reaction as the one before it. How amazing was that?

Harrison's hands expertly roamed over her hips until he smoothly released the garter belt, which he promptly flung aside. His hands returned seconds later to roam her back until her expensive lace bra went flying off as well.

As the constrictions on her now swollen breasts fell away, Harrison's hands replaced the lace. She leaned into his grip on her, closing her eyes, appreciative of the way she felt so womanly under his touch.

"You're so beautiful… I knew you'd be perfect," he whispered.

Doris lost her breath when Harrison's talented mouth swallowed the modest denial she tried to offer. When he finally freed her lips, she undid his cuffs and pushed the shirt off his very wide shoulders. Next she pulled his belt from his already unzipped pants. He helped at the end by pushing them and his briefs down below his hips in one motion, jutting proudly toward her as the expensive clothes fell at their feet.

She'd only been this bold with one man before him, but it was as natural as breathing to indulge her urges tonight. Doris reached out and ran a fingernail from tip to root of his erection, listening to Harrison's breathing quicken as she traced the same path over and over. She was getting dizzier. Soon she would need to lie down.

"Ms. Pearson—do you have any idea what you're doing to me?"

"Yes, Mr. Graham. I believe I do. I am greatly looking forward to accepting the consequences of my actions."

Harrison's hand buried itself in her hair, keeping Doris's very kissable mouth close to his. "You are absolutely the sexiest woman who's ever breathed," he whispered, hissing at the torture she was causing him with every movement of her fingers.

Doris smiled and wrapped her hand firmly around him, using her other to grip his shoulder when he closed his eyes and leaned into her purposeful strokes. Not wanting to end things too quickly, she used her grip to pull Harrison with her. He snickered when she never let go, but eventually fell on top of her when her back hit the king-sized bed.

Somehow her panties disappeared, and along with them, the last of her inhibitions. "Now. Please. Don't wait," she whispered urgently.

But the process of entering turned out not to be so instant. Harrison was big and hard… and she was tight from lack of practice. By the time the initial breech was completed, they were both nearly delirious with the need to chase the fire between them.

The fevered coupling that followed in the next few minutes eventually culminated in her wrapping herself around him like an anaconda. Harrison finally broke one leg's hold and slid a hand under her thigh. He shifted her until she was positioned like he wanted. His movements slowed then to long, deep strokes.

Even in the dark, she could see Harrison watching her expressions. When the pleasure dam broke within her, his own control seemed to break as well. He pushed into her over and over then like he was trying to get inside and stay there. She knew somewhere along the line he'd found his bliss too, but she'd been barely aware of it because he'd ignited a second wave in her with his efforts.

Harrison kissed her endlessly as their heartbeats returned to normal and whispered lovely things while she floated back from where his lovemaking had sent her. When she fell lightly asleep, it was with Harrison still inside her. It was the loveliest feeling in the world to think he didn't want to withdraw. It was also something that had never happened to her before.

The sleep turned out to be a catnap. She was startled to consciousness by Harrison whispering in her ear.

"Still think I'm bragging, Ms. Pearson?"

Doris giggled at his question and what was happening inside her as Harrison got hard again. At least five times this evening, he'd made her feel silly enough to laugh like Vivian. His bragging made her giddy. The man himself made her giddy. She felt young, carefree, and... lucky. Yes, that was how she felt as well. She felt extremely lucky to have Harrison Graham in her bed.

Harrison was obviously ready for round two, but he soon made sure she was as well. His mouth on her breasts pulled the fire up to blazing again in record time. Good lord, the man had stamina. Maybe her sister and her niece were right about younger men.

"Yes, Mr. Graham, I still think you brag incessantly, but now you've convinced me you deserve to do so. In the future, I will refrain from refuting your statements concerning your sexual prowess."

Harrison laughed at her lawyer talk. "About damn time you admitted you like me," he declared. Then he pushed her hair off her face so he could meet her gaze. "I may brag about performance, but I know the real magic takes two people wanting the same thing. You deserve bragging rights yourself, lady. I'll even sign an affidavit if you want. We can post it on the bulletin board at the club if you want to shock the gossip committee."

Doris laughed sincerely. "You're a very tempting man in many ways, Mr. Graham."

When she continued to giggle over their teasing, Harrison rolled until Doris was draped over him like a blanket. She moaned and shifted on his growing erection, kissing his chest as her hips pressed down on his. It was quite the pleasant surprise to discover her enthusiasm matched his so perfectly. The other surprise was when she brought her knees up and rode him hard until they both screamed out each other's names.

When Doris collapsed on him afterward, he didn't care how heavy she was or that she fell immediately sound asleep. He wrapped his arms around her, enjoying the way she felt so right lying on top of him. He wanted to fall asleep while still inside her. Something else he'd never wanted to do before tonight.

One day he was going to make a list of how many firsts Doris had inspired in him.

Harrison raked back her hair and kissed her forehead. "Doris Isette Pearson, I think I might like to marry you one day."

"Whaa…at?"

Exhausted in body and deeply relaxed, Harrison knew Doris hadn't caught what he'd said. Maybe it was a good thing. It spared them both the inevitable fight over his startling intentions. He snickered, rocking them both as he hugged her closer. It had made him feel good to say it aloud.

Beneath him, Doris cleared her throat and raised sleepy eyes to his. He chuckled at the glassiness in her gaze. "Okay, Harrison. Whatever you say. Just don't put the marmalade on until the toast comes out of the toaster," she ordered.

Harrison laughed. "Okay. I promise. Now lay your head back down."

When Doris instantly obeyed, Harrison sighed and stroked her hair. "I suppose I shouldn't be surprised you're bossy in your sleep. Who eats marmalade on toast? Grape jelly, woman. Or strawberry preserves. I'd leave right now if you didn't read the financials every day."

He snorted over his blithely untrue statement and hugged harder. He wasn't leaving. Not ever if he could help it. "How have you reduced me to this? I want to be your damn keeper."

It was her. Just her. Doris was challenging to converse with and yet could be silent without being upset. She teased, taunted, and enjoyed herself in bed in ways he'd never found with any other woman. Doris was simply everything he'd been looking for in a companion and lover.

Which was precisely why he'd fallen head over heels in love for the first time in his life. His grandfather had warned him it would happen this way, but he'd thought maybe he'd inherited his father's bad luck. His possessive feelings about the sexy, older woman draped over him would have made his grandfather very proud.

CHAPTER 7

I T WASN'T THE SHOWER THAT WOKE HIM THE FOLLOWING MORNING, but the absence of the long-legged goddess he'd held all night. He only heard the shower once his brain fog lifted. Then he realized the sun hadn't yet risen outside the windows.

Maybe when Doris finished her morning rituals, she'd come back to bed. He'd love to use his morning enthusiasm to show her how grateful he was for her reciprocity last night. She'd need another shower after he got done with her, but he'd happily help her get clean again.

Floating on his fantasy of morning sex with Doris, Harrison drifted back to sleep for a few minutes. A door opening woke him a second time. Keen disappointment had him scooting up to a seated position when his perfect lover came out of the bathroom dressed in an expensive suit and wearing pearls. She was also wearing a different perfume from last night, one that made him jealous of anyone smelling it other than him. His tongue watered at the thought of exploring her body to find where she'd dabbed it on herself. He'd let her keep the pearls on while he searched. Maybe even her brassiere. For a while anyway.

Harrison shifted position, trying to put aside the fantasy

spinning in his head. Doris's sleek presence was muddling his normally sharp mind. He'd heard of men leveled by great sex, but had never figured on becoming one of them. Now he'd met a woman who could mentally *and* physically cut him off at the knees.

"Good morning," Doris said softly, walking to the closet and pulling out her low heels. "I'm sorry to have to leave so abruptly, but I'm headed to a special court session. I suppose I should have mentioned this last night, but I simply forgot. There's coffee in the cupboard above the coffee pot, and granola and fruit on the counter. Don't feel like you have to rush off just because I do. The Wall Street Journal will get thrown out front around seven. I suggest sitting on the patio to read the paper since you seemed to like it as much as I do. It's beautiful out there this time of day."

Doris tilted her head when Harrison stared at her without speaking. Maybe he wasn't a morning person. He looked like she'd clubbed him over the head.

"I'm sorry, Harrison. I don't do sleepovers, so my manners are probably lacking in morning-after etiquette. Thank you for last night. It was great—*you* were great. Maybe we can do it again sometime when we're both free. I would like that very much."

Harrison was rendered speechless by Doris's unaffected-by-last-night speech. It was the same polite way she offered to meet him for golf again after they hadn't even made it through half the course.

Being without something to say was a situation he seldom allowed to happen to him, especially with women. Damn it. What had he done wrong? Last night was the most incredible night of his life. Doris was acting like their perfect lovemaking happened to her every damn day.

"Did I screw up without realizing it?" he asked, leaning an arm on a knee he'd raised.

The position and the sheet hid his physical reaction to her. Doris's eye roll when she inspected his body language sent his temper rising a notch. Finally, he was seeing a downside to being with someone who was truly intelligent, rather than merely pretending to be. The woman saw through his usual strategies… and obviously wasn't bothered by him sporting a woody she didn't have time for dealing with.

"I can see I've hit a nerve with my directness, so let's do this differently, but we need to be quick," Doris said calmly, taking in a breath. "What were you expecting from me this morning?"

Harrison rubbed his chest. There was a solid lump in the center of it. He'd had her body over and over last night, but now he saw that was all he'd gotten. Sometime during their lovemaking, he'd given her his heart, but Doris had kept hers locked away from what they'd done.

Harrison shrugged a shoulder as he stared. He was tired of hedging. "At the very least, I expected you to fall in love with me and not want to leave my side this morning. Was I reaching too far?"

"Well, I certainly didn't see this coming, especially not from someone with your hit and run record," Doris said.

Harrison felt his face flush when she laughed. Worse, his mind struggled with disbelief as Doris covered her mouth with her hand and sat on a nearby chair.

She was silent while she put on her heels. Harrison suddenly saw the flip side of that admirable quality as well. Finally, Doris cleared her throat, the way she probably did before addressing a jury. He stared into her serene, unfathomable gaze and imagined dragging her back to bed and having his way with her until she lost that haughty, superior expression.

"I'm sorry to have to deliver bad news first thing this morning, Harrison. I'm not like those other divorced women whose beds you've graced routinely since you turned twenty-five. I'm not trying to replace my last husband with someone better. I've made myself a life that doesn't require a man. That's probably too blunt, but that's how I feel."

"Fuck, woman. What's happened to you in your life? That isn't how a woman thinks. That's how a man thinks," Harrison blurted out. He clamped a hand over his mouth to shut himself up. It wasn't how he thought, or at least it wasn't how he thought about being with her. He'd never realized how much his ego was a chest thumping hothead at times.

Doris sighed and sat up straighter. "Maybe you're not as much of an expert on women as you think you are then. Or maybe I just prefer to make up my own mind about what I should think or not think. Does seeing a reflection of your cavalier self in my attitude really bother you that much? I knew when I invited you here that I was going to be the next notch on your divorcee belt. Why should I assume I was any different than the last woman you talked into bed? You're equally charming to everyone."

"No, that's not true…" Harrison stopped when her hand flew up, palm out. Why in hell was he allowing her to shush him? His hand moved to his lap under the sheet to make sure his balls were still attached to his dick.

"My explanation of my feelings wasn't an accusation. Surely you're far too intelligent to penalize me for being a realist. Now, duty calls, and I have to go. This Saturday court appearance is a special arraignment. This particular judge has been known to throw out cases if either attorney isn't in court fifteen minutes before start time. If the docket gets moved, it absolutely won't be because of me."

Doris rose, determined not to overthink her departure. She started to the bedroom door and stopped. She looked at the man who'd done things to her body no other man ever had. Maybe Harrison had a right to think his lovemaking would have brought out the sweet, nurturing female in her. But it just wasn't how she felt this morning. The man had seduced her. She'd seduced him back. In her view, that meant they were even. No harm—no foul.

At the moment, her mind was on needing to be in court… as it should be. She sighed internally, unwilling to let it out and reveal how stressed she was this morning.

She was sure they'd burn out in a few weeks and Harrison would be on to his next conquest. It was what he always did and there was no use pretending he "wasn't like that" the way most women would.

She also couldn't dial back the clock and be as innocent as Vivian merely to soothe his pricked ego. She couldn't do it no matter how talented Harrison Graham was between the sheets.

She resumed her trek to the door. She needed to leave. She needed to clear her head space.

"Doris," Harrison began. "Wait... please... don't run off yet."

When Doris stopped and turned back to him, Harrison sighed at the faux serenity she was projecting. He knew now it covered up a deep disappointment with life in general. How in the world was he going to change her mind after twenty years of her surviving a horrible, unnatural marriage? His gut was screaming at him to correct her wrong assumptions about what they did last night.

"Look—I genuinely, sincerely like you. I wasn't using you last night. You were amazing and this morning you're still amazing. Being with you was so much more than I expected. I don't want to lose what we've barely found. At least tell me we're not over before you go dashing out the damn door."

Doris took in a deep breath and released it slowly. "Okay. I guess I can do that. You're a generous lover, and I know the value of those. During the farce of my legal marriage, I had a romantic relationship with a man named Reynard. He was a proficient, talented lover so I kept going back to him whenever I traveled to Europe. If not for Reynard, I would probably have hated sex forever."

That was news he hadn't needed to hear when his own hard-on for her hadn't yet gone down. Harrison hated thinking Doris had ever found someone better in bed than he was, but he also still wanted to go beat up her ex for being a jerk to her. None of what he was feeling so intensely made sense, based on how little they knew about each other.

"I have no doubt it was Vincent's cheating that drove you to look elsewhere. Why didn't you kick Avery Vincent to the curb and move to Europe? That Reynard guy sounds like he was perfect for you."

Doris studied the wall, firming her mouth. What did she care what Harrison thought about her past? She knew practically everything sordid about his. If he judged her, so what?

"Reynard was perfect for me, but that was because I paid him to be. He worked for an elite escort agency in Paris. I would have had to share him over there just as much as I ever did Avery over here. Reynard was older than me and died two years ago."

Harrison rubbed a hand over his face. He had no problem with her age, but damn that decade between them had chosen to show up in a very strange way. No wonder the other women in his life didn't matter to Doris. Her best experience before him was with a damn French gigolo. Considering the damage Avery Vincent had no doubt inflicted, he was glad to hear there had at least been someone good in her life. There was no road to take but the highest one he could find. All others led away from her. That wasn't something he could bear thinking about after last night.

Harrison firmed his jaw and his resolution. "If you think I'm offended or put off that you went looking for intimacy and comfort from someone better than Avery Vincent, I'm not. I'm also genuinely sorry you lost the man responsible for helping you be the loving version of yourself that I was with last night. Reynard must have been one hell of a guy."

Doris nodded. "He was. And yes, my ability to enjoy you is because of him. Look—I'm sure I'm not the kind of woman you're used to, but you don't have to worry I'll ever expect too much from our time together. When you're done, I'll probably be done too. I'm used to temporary. That's the only kind of sex life I've ever had."

"Up until now," Harrison declared firmly. "You know I have to ask this question. You have money, brains, and nearly all you need to live without a man—as you pointed out. Why did you stay married to a cheating asshole like Vincent all those years once you knew there were better men in the world?"

Doris sighed, and then did something she never did. She shrugged because she was still trying to figure that out herself.

"Staying in loveless relationships is what Pearson women do. They stay with their men no matter how they are treated. And for the first decade or so, I tried everything I knew to make my marriage work. The initial reason I went to Reynard was to see if I could turn myself into a woman Avery might approve of in bed. What I discovered was that I'd married an insensitive jerk who only wanted sex on his terms. Avery didn't care about making love. Reynard told me many times to leave him, but staying married was better for my career choice."

Doris let out the breath she'd been holding. Had she ever said those words aloud before? Probably never. "How about you, Harrison? Why aren't you having your morning conversations with a loving wife? Any woman would marry you… no matter how much you bragged. Once she learned you could make good on your statements, she'd probably do anything you wanted."

Harrison let out a long sigh. "I guess I'm selfish… and cautious. I sought only temporary arrangements because they suited me for the most part. Maybe I've never married because I didn't want to end up repeating my father's life. I've been waiting until I fell genuinely in love, the way my grandparents were."

Doris nodded. "That's an admirable goal. My sister is the only woman in our family who ended up with a real marriage. Avery was a serial cheater and everyone knows that about our relationship, but he treated me well enough to keep in my good graces in every other way."

"Still sounds like a miserable life to me," Harrison declared fiercely.

Doris shrugged a shoulder. "I'm female, Harrison. Bias against my gender is changing, but too slowly to help me live as I pleased. Without being married, my career would never have developed to a point where making law partner was possible. My empty marriage was a Pearson legacy, but one I never felt justified setting aside until I heard about Avery's pregnant girlfriend. Divorce hasn't been as bad as I feared, but I don't ever want to do it again, so remarrying is not a goal for me."

Harrison nodded, not sure of what to say in reply to her negative outlook on relationships. He'd already played his entire hand in confessing how last night spent loving her meant everything to him. Doris's thinking wasn't even in the same place as his so she couldn't hear any of the important things—like the word "love" for instance. He certainly wasn't sure Doris was capable of caring for him the way he did for her, but he wasn't about to give up yet.

"Can we keep dating? I'm specifically talking about an exclusive relationship in the bedroom. Despite what you might believe, I'm not like your ex-husband. I won't cheat on you with other women, but I also don't want to worry that you'll be looking elsewhere either. Usually, I take more precautions in bed. I didn't use any protection with you last night because for once I wouldn't care what happened. I could happily spend the rest of my life with you, Doris. There—that's me being blunt right back."

Doris shook her head. "I got carried away too. What you've shared does make me feel a little less guilty for my lapse in judgment. Since I can't conceive, we're both safe from that scare. I guess being exclusive is fine. When you get tired of warming my sheets, I will still have my life and job and an identity that doesn't end when we do. So long as you don't play any head games with me, we'll get along fine until we're done. And when you move on

—that's it. Don't plan on ever coming back. I will never play second fiddle again."

"Given who you were married to, and what you've told me, I understand your feelings," Harrison declared, but he didn't understand a damn thing actually. At the moment, truly all he wanted was to find Avery Vincent and beat the crap out of him for screwing up the woman of his dreams. "Can I come back tonight?"

Doris shook her head. "I don't think that's a good idea. How about I see you next Tuesday morning on the green?"

"Surely you know this by now... the golf lessons were just a ruse to spend time with you," Harrison admitted.

Doris snorted. "I suspected as much, but you're the first person who's given me a halfway decent game in years. Don't back out on me now, Harrison. You're every bit the outstanding student you promised you were."

Harrison smiled broadly. Please God let that be innuendo, he thought. He needed some small bit of hope. "Okay. I won't back out. I'll be there Tuesday morning."

When Doris nodded, smiled back, and left, Harrison threw the sheet off and stomped into her luxurious bathroom. Like every other room in her large, spacious home, it was decadent too. His problem was that he was in too sour a mood to appreciate the marble counters and gold faucets.

Damn it all to hell. This was the first time he'd ever spent a whole night with a woman and woke up in her bed. Worse... it was the first time he'd ever wanted to.

Chatting up Doris the lawyer this morning while his dick was hard for Doris the woman from last night was not a great way to start a day he'd thought would go a whole lot differently. But the success of his love life had been unpredictable since he'd sat with her at lunch at the club.

He already knew all the cold showers in the world weren't going to erase his need, because his affection for her was growing.

His dick might rise and fall with Doris's receptiveness, or lack of it, but his mind and heart would go on craving more and more of her. He was now officially a one woman man, but ironically he couldn't seem to convince the woman who'd converted him.

Maybe he was doing penance for his father's sins, after all.

Every woman he dated... or slept with... had made him realize finding that one right person was a gift. He'd waited a long time for Doris Pearson. Now, he just had to line up an argument for their continued relationship that the intelligent attorney would accept.

If they married, they could always adopt a child. He'd sell her on that idea later. So what if she was older than him? A decade was nothing these days and she was prime.

But loving him back? That one detail was non-negotiable.

No matter what they never had, Harrison was determined to have her love, her faith, and the rest of her trust. It was simply a matter of time.

CHAPTER 8

Doris put down her fork and sighed in contentment at such a rare Monday treat. Her sister sure knew how to cook. She could cook too, but not nearly as efficiently.

Lunch had been waiting when she arrived at her sister's, but to her credit, Ruth had waited until she'd finished eating before starting the real interrogation.

"Okay, I've fed you and now you owe me. Is it true? That's all I want to know."

Doris narrowed her gaze at her nosey younger sister, but she wasn't seriously mad. Today's interrogation had been as inevitable as Friday night's delicious debauchery.

"Must you always believe the gossip you hear about me?" Doris asked, pretending to be miffed because she knew Ruth would enjoy the drama. She chuckled when her sister smiled.

"Only when I heard it from someone other than the gossip committee, Counselor. In this case, the source was your very own niece. After your cloak and dagger exit from the dance, Lydia Smithfield came back from the gardens, looking stunned. She was the one who told Vivian she saw Harrison Graham kissing you in the gardens. There was something else alarming about where his hands were, but Vivian said Lydia flatly refused to give her any real details."

Doris laughed and rolled her eyes. "Fine. You caught me. Yes, it's true. I kissed Harrison in the gardens. It was in gratitude for letting me take off the damn heels I wore with that green chiffon dress instead of holding me to the dance I'd promised him. That's true gallantry in a man."

Ruth stopped stirring her cookie dough. "Just how grateful were you? I feel like you're leaving out the good parts."

"Why should I discuss this with you? Don't you have a husband you adore?" Doris demanded.

Ruth giggled. "Absolutely. I also have a sister I've been worried sick about. I'd love nothing better than to know you really are kissing a younger man. In fact, I think you should seduce Harrison Graham and let him show you what you've been missing all these years. Just don't get serious about him because he flits from divorced woman to divorced woman without really pausing."

Doris sighed. She'd never told Ruth how she coped in her loveless marriage. She knew her sister likely figured she'd lived like a nun for the last decade, and she'd never corrected that assumption. Mostly she had lived celibately, but Reynard had showed her many ways to tolerate being alone. God bless the man for his tutoring. Otherwise, she might have become as notorious as Avery.

She smiled and nodded at her sister's support. It suited her to let Ruth think Harrison had been the one who replaced Avery's memories. He had been outstanding, and he had replaced memories. Reynard would definitely have approved of him. Odd how knowing that made it easier to confess to her sister.

"If you must know the juicy details of my sordid love life, I invited Harrison home with me after the dance. And yes—he spent the night—the whole night."

The cookie batter spoon went flying. Ruth's stunned open-mouthed stare made Doris belly laugh. She rubbed the indention on her nose where her readers typically rested.

"What? You asked and I told you. I didn't see any reason to wait. Harrison was quite proficient. It was all I could have hoped for and better than I expected. In fact, I've already invited him to come back again."

Doris fell silent as her sister scooped up the dirty spoon from the floor and tossed it into the sink. Neither of them spoke as Ruth fetched a clean spoon from the silverware drawer. Silence reigned as uniform balls of dough were scooped out and arranged in perfect lines on the baking sheet.

"So did you fall in love with him?" Ruth asked carefully.

Doris snickered at the softly asked question, shook her head, and then laughed because the idea of falling in love after one night in bed was as funny as it was unexpected.

"No, Ruth. Of course not. The last thing I want is another Avery in my life, but at least I like Harrison. The man is smart, entertaining company, and I don't have to apologize every two seconds for having my own opinions. I admire that nothing seems to put Harrison off. He's even sending some guy over to fix the door that goes outside to the patio. I'm pretty sure Harrison and I are going to be friends when this is all over. In the meantime, I plan to make the most of my turn with him."

Ruth shook her head as she slid the cookies into the oven and set a timer. "Men don't work like that, Doris. None are rational in their thoughts, and they're all extremists. They either own you completely, or they move on like you never existed. I've seen it time and again. In the last three years, Harrison has slept with Frances Stigner, Eileen Tennyson, Sarah Dunham, and Ginny Wilson who now works full time at the club. They were all perfectly nice women. He didn't keep any of them even though they all wanted to keep him."

Doris shrugged. "He told me he never gets serious. He also told me he tells every woman that up front. I imagine he does, but women bent on nabbing a man rarely listen. If he's being honest, you have to admire him for laying it out straight."

Ruth fisted a hand on her hip. "Unbelievable. So he bragged to you about his previous conquests?"

Doris grinned as she shook her head. Harrison had bragged, but not crudely. "No, Ruth. Harrison is much too smooth for that sort of bragging. He simply told me he's never settled down because he's been looking for a woman to love. I think I believe him. He's manipulative, but he doesn't strike me as being dishonest. Trust me when I say he has no need to be. I think he gets his way because he's so damn nice. The rest of his talents are just a very pleasant bonus. He seems like a decent guy."

"Are you thinking you're going to maybe be his one exception to moving on?" Ruth demanded.

"Don't be ridiculous," Doris replied, huffing at the thought. "I'm a decade older than him. When he's ready to settle down, he's going to pick someone closer to Vivian's age who can still give him a family. You know how the Graham men are about their progeny. His grandfather was so proud of his father and him. Being barren, I'm the last woman in line for the role of Graham wife."

Truly Harrison sticking around hadn't crossed her mind, though Doris was still pondering his insistence on officially declaring that they were in a relationship. That didn't seem to fit his usual hit and run style of seducing women.

Of course, he hadn't really gotten a chance to seduce her. She had sort of beat him to it. Maybe he was hanging around until he'd had a chance to successfully play his conquering game. For some reason, the very thought of Harrison trying to seduce her made her smile. He had been as receptive to her as she'd been to him. She might be naïve, but she wasn't stupid.

"All I'm expecting are a few pleasant sleepovers and a mostly talented golf partner at the club for a couple of weeks. That's about all the staying power Harrison has… or so I've observed. Maybe I'm secretly hoping the man will continue to play golf with me when all other things are over. Our games will give the gossip committee something new to chew on. Maybe they'll leave the rest of my life alone."

Ruth snorted. "You and your beloved golf game. Harrison Graham could throw himself at your feet and beg to make an honest woman of you. All you'd want to know is if he would continue to play golf."

"If you saw him playing with me, you'd understand why I feel like I do," Doris said with a grin.

Ruth giggled. "Is that innuendo, Counselor?"

"Just a hard fact, Mrs. Waterson. Very hard."

"*Doris*… I can't believe you actually said that!"

Doris's laughter over embarrassing her sister echoed through the kitchen. The oven timer dinged and further startled her already surprised sibling. Ruth bent to take the pan of cookies out. Her sister's domesticity suited her perfectly. Doris's amusement faded as she looked at her watch.

"Thanks for the delicious lunch, honey. I have to get back for a meeting. Can I have my dessert to go? The cookies smell so amazing, I have to have a couple."

Nodding, Ruth wrapped several hot cookies in foil. She folded the edges, flattened a piece into a handle, and passed the package over.

Doris giggled as she turned it around in her hands. "Tin foil art. Amazing. Looks like my briefcase."

Ruth laughed. "Yes. I did that on purpose. I know sometimes you think I don't approve of your life, but the truth is I admire you. What you've done is nothing I would have or could have done myself, but I think it's important that you chose what worked for you. So many women get divorced and have nothing left from twenty years of being a wife. I'm glad that's not happening to my sister. I'm glad you have work you like and money enough to take care of yourself."

Doris pressed the warm foil package to her chest. "Since you started this mushy discussion, I will admit that I love you to pieces. Mom and Dad still think I should have kept Avery and paid his child support because his cheating was partly my fault. How degrading would that situation be if I accepted what they said as a truth? It's nice to know my beautiful, talented, and wonderful baby sister doesn't hate me for getting divorced."

"Avery Vincent is a cheating asshole and I'm glad you escaped with your financial life intact. Now go. Don't miss your meeting. Come back and have dinner soon. I'm betting Vivian is going to be announcing her engagement shortly. We'll have a lot of fun helping her plan her wedding."

"I'm not sure I'm up for that much family fun, but thank you for including me, honey." Doris hugged her sister hard, holding her delicious smelling cookies out of the way while Ruth laughed.

THE PHONE RANG INSISTENTLY as he gathered up his car keys and wallet before heading out the door. His answering service notified him via beeper. Giving in, Harrison reluctantly answered, intent on giving the telemarketer a piece of his mind when they asked him if the "lady of the house was home". Reminding himself that it might be his next appointment trying to cancel, he forced himself to politely say hello.

He had dashed home for a quick lunch and was heading to a rendezvous with a realtor he'd met in his favorite coffee shop. He had his eye on acquiring a giant sprawling house she had listed and was more inspired after seeing Doris's. The home was on the market because the couple who owned it were divorcing. Harrison had already settled on an offer in his mind, but he'd thought it best to see the place in person before making it official.

Instead, he found himself rushing to the hospital five minutes later, glad now he'd taken the time to answer the phone. His father's episodes were happening closer and closer together. The man needed to stop drinking. In fact, he needed to stop doing a lot of things.

Harrison found his latest stepmother in the waiting room, adding another coat of paint to her fingernails. Fighting the urge to roll his eyes, he cleared his throat as he approached. Her head came up and a welcoming smile covered her face. The woman was his age. He still couldn't get used to seeing someone that young snuggled up with his father. That was a bias he was going to have to shed if Doris stayed in his life.

"Hi, Angela. How bad is it this time?" he asked.

Angela shook her head and sent her nearly shoulder-length hoops swinging against her long hair. "I'm not sure. The doctors were bustling around like crazy and not talking to me. I would have driven the car home, but the nurses took the keys to the Cadillac. I don't think they like me very much. But don't worry about me, Harrison, your father gave me money. I'm doing just fine. I can take a cab home later if I have to. I thought I would stick around in case someone came out to tell me how he's doing."

Harrison pressed his lips together tightly, fighting the urge to chastise the woman for being practically useless. No one would take Angela seriously enough to give her real information. He shoved his hands into his pockets to help himself think. "I'm going to go see if I can find out anything. The hospital called me about him. That's why I'm here."

"Oh," Angela said, "I guess I should have called you. Sorry about that. I was just so worried."

Harrison nodded. It didn't surprise him. His dad only kept company with one type of woman, and it was not the type who was going to care for him when he got sick. He didn't know what good having a legal wife did his old man. Hospitals still called him because he was listed as next of kin.

"It's okay, Angela. I'll let you know what I find out."

He wandered over to the nurse's station and smiled at the woman behind the desk. Moments later he was peeking around a door at his father who was reclining in the bed. He walked in quietly. His father was staring out of the window and didn't turn until he stood next to the bed.

"Well, it's official, son. I'm really dying this time," Jefferson Walter Graham announced.

Harrison sighed at his father's dramatics. "We all are, Dad. That's just a part of life, isn't it? Grandpa went down swinging. I'm sure you will too."

His father turned a serene and sober gaze in his direction. "I'm not a good candidate for heart surgery, but that's fine with me. I'd rather have a few more good months than several years of struggling to recover from something that can't cure me."

Harrison shrugged. "You could always try giving up cigarettes and booze, Dad. That would probably make you a better candidate for the surgery."

Jefferson snorted. "You know, Harrison—your mother would be thrilled with the way you turned out, especially when you get all self-righteous like this. I know I don't say it often, but I'm proud of you, son. It's a given now that I'm not going to live to see your children, but you should still consider having them. Don't let my bad luck with women stop you. You need a son to leave that fortune you're making to, who will one day appreciate it. Having you all these years has kept me sane."

Harrison thought of Doris… and her childless state. There would be no more biological Grahams if he married her, but this probably wasn't the time to inform his father of his intentions.

"Come on, Dad. Don't talk like that simply because you had another episode. I'm sure you'll live long enough to see me marry. I haven't stopped looking yet," Harrison hedged. He went silent when his father shook his head.

"Not going to happen, boy. They tell me my ticker's nearly

dead already," Jefferson said. "Just know you'll get the lion's share of everything, including the house, when I'm gone. Angela will be taken care of, at least enough to hold her until she finds another man to leech off of."

"That's a hell of a way to talk about your wife." Harrison shook his head as he dropped down into a chair near his father's bed. Instead of slapping him down verbally, his father snickered at his disrespect.

"Angela is company, boy. She's not a real wife. Your mother was my only real wife. I wish like hell I'd been a good husband to her. She deserved a better man than I ever was. She deserved someone like your grandfather. Dad always said he set his sights on Mom and that was it for him. He called it the Graham curse to be so single-minded about a female. I wasn't surprised he died shortly after Mom did. He loved her so much."

Harrison nodded. "Yes, I know he did. He always made her smile, no matter if she was mad or upset or worried. Grandpa would sing or dance, and she would start laughing."

He paused and saw his father looking out of the window again.

"What was the deal between you and Mom? I've never been able to figure it out." Harrison frowned when his father shook his head. "Tell me, Dad."

"Are you sure you want to hear this?" Jefferson asked.

Harrison thought about it because sometimes ignorance really was bliss. "Well, if I can't hear the real truth about the bad marriage of my parents at thirty-three, I need to grow the rest of the way up fast. Tell me."

Jefferson sighed. "Your mother was the perfect woman in nearly every way. She adored me from the beginning, and no one could have asked for a better wife. The problem was that I never felt that way about her. Oh, I liked her. I suppose you can even say that I was fond of her, but I didn't love her. I've never felt the inclination to be monogamous with any woman. I don't think I got that Graham gene that recognizes that one right female. Like you, I never stopped looking, but I guess I have to now. I've run out of time."

"Are you telling me you didn't love my mother? At all?" Harrison demanded, shocked despite telling himself he was tougher than that.

"No, I didn't," Jefferson replied quietly. "At least I never loved her like a woman wants and needs to be loved. I even told her that and gave her the chance to leave me. She said she wanted to stay with me—then with you too after she got pregnant. I let her stay, even when I knew it wasn't fair to do so. Just before she died, she told me she still had no regrets. Ironically, regrets are all I do have now that she's gone. The other women are because I don't want to die alone the way your mother did."

Harrison leaned forward and rested his elbows on his knees as he studied the floor. His insides were churning. He wished now he hadn't eaten lunch.

"Do you hate me for not loving your mother the way I should have?" Jefferson asked.

Harrison shook his head slowly from side to side. "Mom used to tell me it wasn't my business to fix your relationship with her. Mostly I feel sorry for you never feeling that level of love, and I'm slightly mad at Mom for staying with someone who didn't love her. But I do understand neither of those are really my business. You each chose to live in the way that suited you. I'm old enough to accept that, so I will."

Jefferson lifted a finger and pointed it, narrowing his gaze. "And that is why you will accomplish any damn thing you want in life, boy. You are accepting of people's weaknesses, even though I know damn well you use that understanding to get your way when it suits you to do so. Hands down, creating you was the best thing I ever accomplished, including all the money I made over the years. I may have been a shitty husband to your mother, but I worked at being a good father. It was the only way I was ever able to make all of us happy."

Harrison drew in a breath. He hadn't been happy with his father's efforts at parenting. His father had been absent more than home, but you couldn't say such things to your potentially dying parent.

"You were better than many fathers I knew," he offered, lifting his gaze. "Dad, are you really dying?"

Jefferson chuckled and then sighed heavily. "Yes, son. I really am. Talk to Dr. Spencer. He'll tell you all about it. He wants me off cigarettes and booze. I told him I might as well be buried tomorrow."

Harrison leaned back in his chair. "Try to live as long as you can, okay? I'm not ready to inherit your wealth. I'm still busy trying to prove I can make my own damn money."

Jefferson laughed as he leaned back. "You are so much like my father. I bet one day some woman is going to come along, and that will really be it for you. If you'd lay off those swinging divorcees and date some good girls, you might find your perfect wife a tad faster."

Harrison rose, saying nothing. He was not discussing Doris with a man who dated women his age and younger. "I'm going to find the doctor. You want me to send Angela in?"

Jefferson shook his head and snatched his car keys off his nightstand. Harrison barely caught them when they were thrown his way.

"Here. Send Angie home. There are a couple cute nurses who like my company more than she does. Angie might as well watch TV and talk to her girlfriends until I get sprung. Tell her to bring me back some clothes tomorrow when she comes to get me. There's nothing more they can do, so they're going to let me go home."

Harrison closed his hand around the keys. "Okay," he whispered, reality sinking in.

He walked out of the room thinking about what it would be like if his father really did die. It wasn't like they were close, but the man was all the family he had left. His grandparents had died just before his mother. He was worn out with all the loss he'd had in the last five years.

And right now he really needed to talk to someone about this latest shock.

CHAPTER 9

WHEN THE DOORBELL RANG, DORIS WAS IN THE KITCHEN. SHE looked down at her sweatpants and sighed in frustration. She'd didn't want to answer the door like this.

Actually... she didn't want to answer the door at all.

Her monthly cycle, though not as regular since she turned forty, was going to start soon. No matter that her personal calendar said it was not due yet, she was bloated and irritable and far too hormonally grumpy for talking nicely to company. She'd even left work early this afternoon, hoping for a quiet evening at home where she could feel sorry for herself until she got over it.

Trudging reluctantly to the front door, she peered through the peephole and swore in a whisper. Her stomach fluttered with a foreign excitement which was probably the best reason she had for ignoring her unexpected visitor. She'd been moments away from calling to cancel their golf game tomorrow morning because she simply wasn't up to dealing with it or him.

Now Harrison stood on her front step, and she stood in her hallway wondering how to handle his unexpected appearance. She supposed she could pretend not to be home. It was possible he'd be polite and leave. Since she couldn't decide why she felt the need to ignore him instead of confront him, Doris pulled the door open just to stop the crazy avoidance urge dead in its tracks.

"Harrison? What a surprise," Doris lied, blinking innocently at him. Ruth and Vivian both would have been so proud of her feigned politeness.

When Harrison looked guilty and shoved his hands in his pockets, her resolve to send him away wavered. He stood there obviously trying to think of a polite lie himself, and suddenly she couldn't stand it anymore. Mentally kicking her manners in the ass, she smiled bravely at him.

"Come in... please. I was just about to pour myself a glass of wine and head out to the patio. You're welcome to join me."

Harrison shook his head and looked off to the right. "Before I say yes—and I really want to say yes—I want you to know that I didn't come with anything in mind except to talk. I needed not to be alone this evening. You're the only person I felt like seeing."

Doris nodded at his honesty and returned the favor. "Okay. Well, I'm not really in the mood to do any entertaining tonight, but I might manage to be a sloppily dressed friend who listens."

Harrison snickered at her qualifying statements, but he crossed Doris's threshold and counted himself lucky she let him in at all. "You could just stand there and glower at me for being a rude asshole who didn't call before stopping by. Even if you did that, I'd still consider you entertaining. I'm sorry to interrupt your evening plans."

"Yes... well, you caught me in my sweats. If you stay, I'm not changing."

"Deal," he said.

Doris hung her head and chuckled when Harrison grinned at her. He was saying a lot of polite words, but somehow she knew he had something less polite on his mind. She hoped like hell it wasn't having a discussion about them because she hadn't made up her mind yet if she wanted there to be a "them" or not.

She dropped her gaze away when she realized she was staring

hard at him. Maybe she was jaded from too many years of legal clients who said one thing while meaning another.

Harrison's woodsy aftershave wafted by her nose as he walked by. Suddenly, she wanted to hug him and be hugged back. The urge stayed with her and made her sigh when he stopped just a few feet away. His masculinity always reached out to her. He appealed to her physically and her mind went back to Friday night, revisiting it against her will. She shook her head to shake off her thoughts.

"I had no real plans this evening, just a few loose intentions to pamper my bad mood. I'm miserable in both body and spirit, but I'm making ham sandwiches. Want one? I can even do pickles and chips."

"Sure… sounds great… if it's no trouble," Harrison said politely, trailing behind her swinging hips.

He noticed her bare feet made no sound on the tile extending from the hallway to the kitchen. The sweatpants on her hips were loose and hung low on an ample rear that he instantly recalled fitting his hands perfectly. His mind started wondering about her underwear status under the thick gray material before he wrenched it viciously back to the present. He'd told her he had not come to lust. He had to at least attempt to keep his word.

"Did you have a bad day at work?" he asked.

Doris shook her head as she pointed to a seat at her kitchen bar. She'd always loved the casual seating in the room. A long time ago, so long she barely remembered, she'd hosted parties and fed guests at the bar. Now one lone, nearly solemn man sat waiting for her to feed him. He looked like he needed comfort food as much as she did, though why she felt his hunger was her responsibility to solve, she didn't know.

"Today was no worse than usual," she said, heading to the refrigerator. She pulled sandwich makings from it then set them on the counter next to a loaf of bread. "I'm just feeling a bit under the weather, woman wise. I was going to call you to cancel our game tomorrow morning. I don't think I'm physically feeling up for it."

"Me neither," Harrison declared, sighing at the truth. "I just came from the hospital. My father's in there because of his heart. The prognosis is not good. They don't know how much time he has left."

Doris stopped making the sandwich. She moved down the counter, poured a glass of wine for Harrison, and then carried it to where he sat. Setting the glass down, she pushed it away for a moment, then put her arms around him, and leaned against his chest. She hadn't had much practice at comforting people she cared about, but as his arms came tightly around her, she knew she'd done the right thing in offering the hug she'd wanted as well.

"I'm sorry about your father. If there's one blessing in my life, it is that my parents take good care of themselves. That's probably the biggest upside to them belonging to the country club."

Harrison nodded against her shoulder. "Dad drinks and smokes and sleeps around every chance he gets, even when he's married. He won't give any of it up, not even to live longer. There's nothing I can do about his choices, but it seems a shame. My Grandfather Graham lived to be ninety-four."

Doris pushed away and ran a hand through his hair while she looked into his troubled eyes. "And you'll probably live that long as well since you barely take two sips of any wine I pour for you. However, I'd never ask you to give up sex. It's probably healthy for your body to keep sleeping with someone whenever you can. I know it certainly helps me."

He snorted at her crude teasing and rolled his eyes. But he couldn't say anything because he'd started it. "Unlike my father, I believe my sleeping around days are now behind me."

Doris patted his chest and pulled slowly away. She scooted the wine closer to him and then headed back to their sandwiches.

"My memory isn't that bad yet. You're an outstanding lover. Unless you believe in the concept of carnal sin, I don't think you have anything to worry about except living as good a life as possible. That will keep you mentally sound."

"I know I can't change the state of my father's mind. My mother tried, but it never took. To this day, I don't know why she stayed married to him. He's an okay father, but he's a real horse's ass to women."

Doris frowned as she tightened her jaw but kept her head turned away so Harrison wouldn't see. Her hands layered on meat, cheese, and crisp vegetables. She made his bigger even though they were nearly the same size human beings. The whole man-woman thing was deeply ingrained in her and some habits were simply too hard to break.

"I handle a lot of divorces at work. Nine times out of ten it's the man who's wanting out of the relationship. For the most part, women are programmed to stay. My family stopped me from leaving Avery. Maybe your grandparents stopped your mother from leaving your father. It's usually a mistake to put all the blame on one person."

Harrison shook his head, though she never turned to see him do so. "No. My maternal grandparents would have supported her leaving, at least before I came along. My paternal grandparents were constantly on my father's ass about treating her better. Their chastisement didn't help either. I can only conclude that my mother loved him as much as Dad said she did. But he told me this afternoon that he never loved her back. He said he's never loved any woman."

"That's a common plight, but still a sad one, especially for you being their child." Doris piled a handful of chips next to each sandwich. She tucked two cloth napkins under her arm and carried their food plates with her. "Open the door and then grab my glass too. Let's go outside."

Harrison popped the door open with a single shove of one of his wide shoulders against it. She tried not to think about his strength and how sexy she found it. He held the door open as they exited, then he gently closed it most of the way. He left the door jamb unstuck and loose so they could get back inside easily. It was her trick too.

Sighing at the ease between them she couldn't really explain, she sat the plates across from each other on the table. Harrison delivered wine glasses to their perspective places and sat obediently. She crunched a chip and swallowed before speaking to him again.

"I've never been in that kind of love either," she confessed finally. "Have you?"

The chip Harrison put in his mouth was suddenly dry as dust. He stared into sharp green eyes and wondered why Doris couldn't read what was in his gaze. The woman made him feel naked emotionally. Maybe it didn't show, but he'd find that surprising if true, considering how strangely content he felt being with her. "No. I haven't loved anyone… up to now."

Doris picked up another chip, crunched it, and swallowed. "Well, you have plenty of time. Hell, I have time. People fall in love at all sorts of ages. Besides, I can't give up looking for a man who will make me happy. Vivian made me promise not to. I can't seem to convince her or my sister that I can get by just fine on my own."

"My biggest problem is that the Graham men are all cursed," Harrison declared, grinning when she gave him a disbelieving look. "No, I'm serious. My paternal grandfather warned me. He said it had been happening for generations. My father—his son— seems to be the only exception so far. Graham men fool around and live the free life for a long while and then BAM… they find the right woman and that's it. They're married for the rest of their life."

Doris shrugged and took a bite of her sandwich. After she swallowed, she spoke again. "That's not a curse, Harrison. It sounds like the male reality every woman in the world believes and yet dreams of changing by being *the one*."

"Really? Is that your dream?" Harrison asked.

Doris laughed from her belly. It eased a tension she hadn't realized she'd been carrying around. Their verbal sparring was better than watching television, which she still couldn't say she enjoyed. "When I chose to have a career that required I speak my true mind on things, my coy feminine wiles evaporated and never returned. I became a feminist in my choices, but especially about career equality because it was logical."

"I hear a big BUT in that explanation. Rational decision making is not a fault in your character. Nor is it the property of women labeling themselves as feminists. Men have no such labels," Harrison insisted.

Doris shrugged one shoulder. "Feminism is a courage word women adopted so they have a better societal response. How it is viewed depends on how it manifests in a woman's life. Underneath my decision to stay married, I knew I was merely creating a cover story for my toxic relationship. Leaving you in bed to go to court Saturday morning—that was the real me. I work hard, and try to play hard when I can, because I like playing with men. But I was never a woman like Vivian or my sister. I like taking care of myself. I'm not dependent on anyone."

Harrison focused on his sandwich and wondered why her independence was the one part of her speech that bothered him. "Thanks for feeding me. I didn't eat much lunch because I expected to take my realtor to dinner this evening."

"Oh? Hot date?" Doris asked, swallowing down the bite that nearly got stuck in her throat.

Harrison stopped eating and narrowed his eyes. Why would he come to her if that was the case? What kind of opinion did she secretly harbor about him? "Stop with the tone and the eluding. I already told you my sleeping around days are behind me. Actually, I'm buying a house, or trying to, but I want it a hell of a lot cheaper than they're asking. I was going to take the realtor to dinner to try and talk her down on the price."

Doris chuckled. "I see. Well, you did warn me that Monday

was your most ruthless day of the week. Just what kind of leverage were you intending to offer the woman?"

Harrison snorted. "I would have found out what she and the seller wanted most and given her that."

Doris laughed. "An explanation which surely excuses my eluding tone from earlier," she countered.

"No, it doesn't. If you knew me better, you would know I would never sell my manly services as part of a business deal. That would make me too much like all of my stepmothers," Harrison said back, waving a hand. "And it's just plain lazy. When I make a deal, there are no strings attached to me personally. The only money I make is the guilt-free kind."

"Given how well you proved your bedroom bragging, I'm just going to believe your business skills are equally daunting and carry the same integrity. Mostly I say this because I can't afford to lose any more possessions. I'm still recovering from a nasty divorce."

"Doll, you're sitting on the only possession you own that I'm interested in."

"Yes, I know," Doris said sadly. "I saw you mooning over these patio chairs before you even slept with me. I should have known better than to misinterpret your lustful motives."

Harrison snorted. "It wasn't *just* the chairs I was lusting after."

"Damn it, Harrison. You want the table too? Are you always such a greedy bastard?"

His face almost hurt from smiling so hard at her. "You have no idea how greedy I can be about what I want, Ms. Pearson, but I'd sure love to show you."

Doris grinned. "Unfortunately, there's that horrible bragging thing you do—very off-putting."

"You may be a pro on the golf course, but you need to keep in mind that I'm the pro in the bedroom. I don't remember you complaining about my techniques last Friday night. Can you deny my expertise, Counselor?"

Doris giggled and shocked herself. "Just because I can't deny it doesn't mean the jury isn't still out about its long-term benefits, Mr. Graham. Sometimes evidence can be deceiving. A person often has to go a little deeper to find the truth."

"Fine. I'm more than happy to go as deep as you want… and I come equipped to do so. Just say the word."

"Braggart. Braggart. Braggart," Doris chanted.

A potato chip flying across the table bounced off his chest. Harrison smiled around the next big bite he took while Doris continued to laugh over their flirting.

CHAPTER 10

Panting hard as she stared at her bedroom ceiling, Doris covered her still tingling breasts with her own hands. Harrison's evening growth of beard had been tantalizing but she would probably be sporting a rash over her entire chest tomorrow.

She groaned when the man next to her knuckle stroked the sparse curls at the junction of her thighs, barely skimming another part of her that was still tingling. He leaned over and kissed her stomach, then repeated the stroking action a few more times as he continued to kiss around her navel.

"I swear you're the sexiest woman I've ever known. We barely get finished, and all I can think about is starting all over again."

His sincerity sent tingles of arousal shooting outward until they had spread from head to toe. Her groan of approval for it sent him scrambling up her to claim her mouth again.

She felt like one live wire beneath Harrison's talented hands. The heat he generated inside her centered in her middle, right under where his lips like to press. Hormones that had been torturing her for days were completely forgotten in the afterglow of his lovemaking. Who knew multiple orgasms could cure PMS? She wondered if any other female knew this secret.

"Showoff," she rasped out through a throat dry from calling his name over and over. Harrison had been relentless in pleasuring her. She wanted him to be that way again. It was her worst fear come true to long for him.

His groan as his hand slid possessively down and around one thigh had her nearly whimpering. She felt him stir against her leg, stunned at his rapid recovery.

"Really?" she asked in disbelief, her voice nearly squeaking.

"Not really," he answered with a laugh. "It's just still hard from last time. Want to go again and see if it will work?"

"Are you kidding? I still don't know how I ended up naked with you tonight."

Harrison drew in a sharp breath, but let his hand continue roaming. "Well… I was carrying dishes to the sink and you had your back to me. I looked at your awesome butt in those sweats and I just had to have it."

"Yes… had to have it bent over the sink, as I recall," Doris said dryly.

"Yes. I'm sincerely glad you're not short. That was perfect."

Doris giggled insanely. He was right. It had been perfect. "I've never managed to get there in that position before you. Congratulations on your technique."

"Really?" Harrison said, nudging her hand away so he could nibble on a taut rosy bud. "Is that why you were screaming my name loud enough for the neighbors three houses down the street to hear?"

She shoved hard and manage to push his laughing ass off her. "Braggart."

Harrison put his hands behind his head. "Not if it's fact."

Growling, Doris rolled and dove on top of him. She pushed down his shoulders and had a knee pressed against his precious man jewels before he caught on he was in trouble. When his dick twitched again, she laughed and climbed off. He might be a braggart, but he had great follow-through on what he said. She couldn't dispute it.

"You bent me over the sink, and I wasn't even sure I wanted this to happen again, period," she complained.

Harrison chuckled. "Sure could have fooled me. You were wet and hot and… damn, woman. I can't stay out of you when you start arguing with me."

"Oh, shut up. Women get horny too you know. I guess I was needy tonight."

"Yeah, but women usually don't tell you that stuff… or show you. And most don't even move under you even when you're busy doing all the work they like."

Doris snorted as she turned her head to glare. "Do you mind if we skip the play by play description of your previous women in bed?"

Harrison crawled on top of her and tried to stop his mouth from twitching. "I'm trying to offer you a compliment. You're the best lover I've ever had. Can you just take it for what it is and say thank you?"

"Well, what does your opinion of me in bed have to do with anything?" Doris demanded. "I can tell you like having sex with me, despite the fact that you don't always finish when I do."

Harrison stared and realized she was as dense as she was intelligent. "It's important because I'm not done with you, and I don't want this relationship to end. Do you?"

"No," Doris said softly, going still beneath his grip. "Who said anything about it ending?"

Harrison put his forehead on hers as he parted her legs to rest his erection between them. He wasn't letting her pull away or hide in modesty. He wanted her, all of her, especially the parts no one else had appreciated. Like the way she responded to him so completely.

"I'm just worried. I like you, Doris. I don't want you to think I'm just screwing around… no matter how well I do it."

When her eyes darkened, Harrison released a wrist and clapped a hand over her mouth.

"No," he warned, laughing nervously. "No… now that wasn't bragging. I know it sounded a bit like it, but I swear on a stack of Bibles that it wasn't meant that way. I'm not half as cocky as you keep accusing me of being."

Doris felt her mouth twitch under Harrison's hand and then suddenly she was laughing. She didn't even know why she found his denials so funny. When his hand slid away, her laughter echoed in the room.

Harrison growled in her ear as he slid inside her again. She wrapped herself around him as her laughter faded into the most profound sense of belonging she'd ever known. For the first time since she talked to him, she wondered what it would be like to have Harrison in her life all the time.

The next orgasm he gave her sent her into a bout of unexplainable weeping. After her lover found his bliss too, he held her tightly until sleep claimed the rest of her crazy thoughts.

She woke at her regular time the next morning, tangled in crumpled bed sheets and smelling like a mixture of Harrison's aftershave and sex. Her body was far more at ease today, though, and she thought she might be able to survive going into work after all.

If she'd known his lovemaking was going to cure her monthly torture, she wouldn't have called off their golf game.

A quick trip to the kitchen to retrieve her abandoned sweats confirmed there was no sign of Harrison anywhere. Perhaps she should have been worried, but she wasn't. Grateful for his absence and the blissful peace he'd left behind, Doris took her well-used body to the bathroom to start her day.

⁓

SHE WAS HUMMING at her desk and organizing her next court case when the firm's office manager abruptly came into her office and closed the door.

"I'm sorry to barge in, Doris," Karen stated, wringing her hands. "But I couldn't call you about this over the intercom. I knew that would be... bad."

Doris's eyebrows rose. "Sounds intriguing. What's going on?"

Karen put her hand on her chest and drew in a breath. "Your ex-husband is here. He wants to see you about representing him in a legal matter."

Doris sighed but shrugged. Avery probably wanted to change his will to make sure she was no longer in it, but she wasn't willing to do any more work for him. "Fine. Let him come back. I'll get rid of him as soon as I can."

Karen was shaking her head, her curled bob not even moving with the motion. Doris never understood how the woman's hair could stay in place so well. No hairspray was that strong. She had to touch up her French twist two or three times a day.

"You don't understand, Doris. You need to know this before you see him... Avery wants you to handle his divorce from his new wife. Isn't she pregnant? I thought they were having a baby."

Doris froze in place, blinking rapidly, as if that would change what she heard. "Are you sure that's what Avery wants?"

Karen nodded. "I asked in several different ways to make sure I'd heard him right."

Doris dropped her chin, pondered the problem, and then lifted it. "Representing him would be a conflict of interest, even if I were interested, which I most certainly am not. I can't believe he'd do this to her while she's having his child. No attorney will want to take the case until the baby is born."

Karen nodded vigorously. "I know. So what do you want me to do with him?"

Doris sighed heavily. "He'll get whiny if I refuse to see him and kick up a fuss. Send him back before Larry or Edward find out

he's here. They teased me enough over handling my own divorce.
I don't want Avery coming to me for his next divorce to be the
thing they laugh about at the Christmas party this year."

"Oh, Doris... I'm so sorry," Karen declared in a soft whisper.

Doris laughed. "I'm joking. It's not that bad. Send him back so
I can get rid of him."

Karen disappeared and returned in under a minute.

Doris settled her readers on her nose as Avery came into her
office. "Hello, Avery. I hear you're looking for legal
representation."

Avery shrugged and took one of the chairs facing her desk.

"You've redecorated since the last time I was here," he said,
looking around the room.

Doris peered over her readers giving him a look. "The last
time you came to my office was more than a decade ago. You
asked me to move back into the master bedroom. I said no. My
answer is going to be the same today. Whatever it is... the answer
will be no."

Avery held out both hands and smiled. "You don't even know
what I want."

"Unfortunately, I do. Karen told me. It's her job to filter what
comes through my door."

"I know you don't think too well of me right now, but you
could at least hear my explanation."

Doris snorted. "What viable explanation could you have for
trying to divorce the mother of your unborn child? No attorney
will take that on because no judge would be willing to hear the
case. You're going to have to at least wait until after the child
comes... typical advice is to wait at least a year for propriety's
sake."

"Oh." Avery rubbed his chin. "I never thought of that."

"Yes... well, the real time for thinking was before you
unzipped your pants."

Avery chuckled. "Same old Doris. You still don't pull any

punches."

Doris folded her arms on top of her desk and leaned forward, glaring at him over her glasses.

"Coming here was short-sighted. One—because I would never, ever handle your divorce from another woman for any reason. I'd be more apt to handle hers. And two—because it would be a conflict of interest for me, which means I can't ethically do so, even if I was willing. Both situations would be bad for your case. Larry and Edward will refuse because of their connection to me. So you're going to have to go elsewhere, Avery. Frankly, it's just shitty of you to do this to a woman only a couple months away from giving birth."

"Do you have any respect for me at all?" Avery asked.

"No. None."

He rose from his chair. "Well, I won't waste any more of your time then."

Doris nodded. "I will advise you to reconsider this course of action. Your reputation won't survive abandoning your child."

Avery paused at the door. "The baby is not my child."

"Why would you say that?" Doris demanded. She saw Avery open his mouth, reconsider what he might have said, and then close it again.

"All I can tell you is that I'm nearly a hundred percent sure a paternity test would show I am not the father."

"You do realize that sort of testing is very expensive, don't you? And not all courts are even willing to recognize the results. When a legally married wife has a child, the legal husband of that union is considered the official father of record. You would need the actual biological father to come forward to prove differently. All parties would have to sign an affidavit and you would have to waive all future rights to the child while he would take them on in your stead."

"Even Celeste doesn't know who the real father is. She keeps saying it's me."

Doris rolled her eyes. "Because it is you, Avery. Women tend to know these things."

"No. It's not me, Doris. I married her because she was good in bed and her family was loaded. I know you think that's bad, but now I know why I was the first one to attempt making my connection to her legal. She's hell to live with, and now I see that the baby is just going to make things much worse. I thought I could do this for the money, but I can't."

"*Money?* You married Celeste for her money?" Doris held up a hand to calm herself and stop Avery. "No. I don't want to hear this. I don't care. Your life is really none of my business. Go back to your wife and patch things up before the baby comes. It deserves a father who cares. That's all I have to say."

Avery sighed. "I don't know why you're still so angry at me. Aren't you sleeping with Harrison Graham? He's just as bad about women. I'm shocked you'd be seen in his company. The man is bad for your reputation."

"We shared a dance last Friday. I might even go so far as to call us friends. And not that it's any concern of yours—I'm giving Harrison golf lessons."

Avery laughed. "Golf lessons. Right. All I'm saying is that you need to be extra careful with Harrison Graham. He's an infamous hit and run with newly divorced women. Everyone knows that."

"Including me," Doris agreed. "I have no illusions about the man. Now goodbye, Avery. Please don't come back to the office again. There's really no reason for you to do so. Next time I'm going to call security and have you thrown out."

"Doris, I… never mind. It's not important, and it's obvious you don't want to hear it anyway. Have a nice life."

"Try Lighthouse and Williams for your future legal needs. We refer people to them all the time."

She sighed in relief when Avery lifted a hand and walked out of the door. She hoped Harrison was having a better day with his father.

CHAPTER 11

IT WAS AMAZING WHAT KIND OF DIFFERENCE A GOOD RELATIONSHIP could make in a person's life. She found it amazing that Harrison didn't seem to mind if she was dressed up or wearing comfort clothes. It was the happiest she'd ever been with a man's company.

Doris glided into the club just minutes before she was due for lunch. Peering into the dining room, she spied her parents already waiting at the table. They were smiling and talking, looking as relaxed as they always did. She wasn't fooled, but even at her age, she hadn't stopped hoping they would someday move into acceptance of her independent streak.

Taking a deep breath, she braced herself and walked over to them.

"Hello," she crooned, bending down to brush a brief kiss across her mother's cheek.

"Hi, Doris. Thank you for indulging us, honey. We've missed you," Caroline Pearson declared.

Doris walked around the table and hugged her father, who hugged back tightly. "Hi, Daddy."

"Hi, Miss Lawyer Lady," Dennis Pearson said.

Doris smiled. He'd been calling her that since college. "My real title is the Honorable Ms. Doris Pearson."

"Perfect segue, darling. Your honor is exactly what we want to talk to you about," Caroline sang out sweetly.

"No, that's what *you* want to talk to her about," Dennis declared. "I'm just happy to see my daughter looking so good. Look at her, Caroline. Your daughter is glowing with health. Isn't that the most important thing?"

Caroline reached over and patted her husband's hand. "Women bordering on the change often appear in good health, Dennis, then it all goes south once they hit their late forties. Doris is glowing because she always has a shiny face. You know she doesn't believe in over-using her face powder."

Nervous now, Doris felt her gaze bouncing back and forth between her crazier than usual parents. She'd take a hostile witness yelling at her any day of the week. "If this is going to be another lecture about swearing in the dining room, I'll just head on back to work before I swear again because of you two."

"No, this is not a lecture about your language," Caroline declared. "That's old news now. All is forgiven. The fines are paid. We can hold our heads up once more."

Doris watched her mother draw in a breath as she prepared to get down to the real reason for the lunch invitation. "Mother, I'm not discussing my divorce again. It's over and done."

"Now, Doris…" Caroline began.

"Mother… Avery's married to a woman who is having his child. There's no hope of us getting back together. That ship has sailed so far out of port you can't even see it on the ocean."

Her mother nodded briskly. "Of course. I know that now, dear. This is not about Avery."

Doris spread her hands in the air just as the waiter appeared. She lowered them to order a salad and an iced tea. She'd come in here ravenous, but her mother's conversation had already robbed her of her appetite.

Her father turned to her and lifted his chin. "Sweetie, your mother's worried about you dating Harrison Graham. We don't think he's good enough for you. His track record with women is not good."

Doris paused in unfolding her napkin. In slow motion, she finally dragged the pristine white cloth across her skirted lap. "Who told you I was dating Harrison?"

"It's obvious, darling. You left together after the dance two weeks ago. Everyone is talking about the two of you now," her mother declared.

Doris frowned. "We left at the same time, Mother. How does that simple act lead everyone to the assumption we're dating. It's illogical."

"Are you dating him?" her father demanded. "Just tell us the real story so we can field the gossip and put it to rest."

"Harrison and I are friends," Doris hedged. "He's going to plane off the bottom of my patio door to keep it from sticking, and I'm giving him golf lessons. What is everyone's problem with us?"

"You know mixed gender golf games are frowned upon here at the club," Caroline said. "They could lead to all sorts of improper complications. It's simpler to play with someone more your equal."

"No one at this club is my golf equal." Doris huffed out a breath, trying to calm herself. "Mother, I'm forty-three, not twenty-three. This discussion is making me more angry than I can tell you. I do not make life decisions based on gossip here at the club. If I did, I would have divorced my cheating husband the second year we were married instead of waiting until six months ago when I had evidence to justify it."

"Doris… please. Lower your voice."

Doris stood and placed her napkin beside her empty plate. It was a new record. She'd only lasted ten minutes into the inquisition about her dating life. No wonder she'd become a master at legal rebuttal. Her mother had given her plenty of practice in her life.

"Daddy, it was good to see you. Tell everyone to mind their own business about Harrison and me. I don't pick my friends, or my dates, based on what other people say about them. If I did, I definitely wouldn't pick you two as parents because you always have secret agendas for our lunches, but there you are. We work with what we're given in life."

"Now, sweetie…"

Doris held up a hand. Her gaze narrowed on both her parents as they fell silent. "Who I sleep with is my business and mine alone. I'm sure Harrison would be mortified to know my parents have stooped to gossiping about him like everyone else does."

She turned a full glare on the woman who swore she had given birth to her. "Mother, there's more to life than what happens at this country club. Or at least there's a hell of a lot more to *my* life."

She walked away quickly before she said anything worse.

DORIS DIDN'T HEAR from Harrison for nearly five days. She figured the gossip committee had somehow gotten to him as well. Not wanting to let the tongue waggers get by with their mischief, she called his answering service and said she was free for golf on Friday morning. They called her back almost immediately and confirmed his acceptance of her offer.

Feeling like a bloody idiot for chasing after a man who'd left her bed days ago without a freaking word, she dressed in her most casual clothes and headed to the club for their game. She booked their green fees, paying with her credit card. Lloyd was his usual chatty self, but her concern kept her from enjoying it as much as she usually did.

She sighed and leaned on the counter. "Can I ask you something embarrassing, Lloyd?"

Lloyd laughed. "Would this be whether or not I've been grilled about how often you and Mr. Graham show up to play golf together?"

Doris snorted. "You got it. Are my parents doing the grilling?"

"Oh no, Ms. Pearson. It was discreetly done by accounting because they weren't seeing your games show up on your account as charges."

"Oh lord... they busted my system. I thought I was safe." Doris groaned and Lloyd chuckled in response.

"I did have to show the books, since they are open and all. I told them it was highly entertaining to watch you giving Mr. Graham lessons and that both of you were quite polite in moving on as other golfers advanced on the course."

Doris smiled. "Thank you, Lloyd. I hate people being in my business. I can't tell you how much I hate it."

"They're just being nosey, Ms. Pearson. What are they going to do about any of it? Nothing. You just keep on being yourself. I'll keep booking you."

"You are absolutely the best person who works here," Doris said. "If you ever need a reference, you just let me know."

"Thank you, Ms. Pearson. I'm quite happy here. The gossip is always juicy... or so I've heard."

Doris laughed at his teasing until Harrison came in wearing the same man's polo she was wearing and in the same color. She heard Lloyd laughing loudly as he turned his head away from them.

"Great minds obviously think alike," Harrison exclaimed, barely fighting off his appalled reaction to their matching shirts.

"Yes. Let's go with that," Doris declared, already envisioning what the gossip committee was going to say about their matching clothes. "Lloyd... tell this story well, will you?"

"Yes, ma'am. Shall I describe your shirts as lavender or lilac?"

"Storyteller's pick," Doris declared, pushing off the counter. She was already tired and they hadn't even gotten out on the course yet. "I paid the green fees. Will you get us a cart this morning? I'm not up to hauling my bag around today."

Harrison nodded, studying her with concern. "Sure. You okay, Doris? More bad days at work?"

Doris shook her head and let her gaze slide to Lloyd. Harrison caught on quickly and paid for a cart for them. Outside he loaded their clubs into the back and strapped them down.

"You drive," she ordered.

Harrison nodded and grinned. "I was already planning to."

She snorted and glared. "Weren't you even going to ask me?"

"Not when you look like warmed over shit," Harrison declared. He glanced at her shirt, confirming it was *exactly* like his. "Don't you have any blouses for women?"

"None that let me swing a golf club with any real freedom of movement, jackass."

Harrison looked away and laughed as he started the cart. "Okay. I've been called worse, but nothing I deserved quite so much. I don't really care what you wear, you know. My mind has memorized what's under it. I can think of you naked any time I want. I'm just going to do that this morning."

"Get that house you were after?" Doris asked.

"I'm hearing that ominous tone again. What's the house got to do with anything?" Harrison demanded.

"You snuck out of my bed and disappeared without leaving a note. I figured that was Graham goodbye code to let me know you were moving on so you could get your deep discount from your realtor woman."

"Well, I'll be damned. This is about my past, isn't it?" Harrison asked with a heavy sigh.

"No. It was only about your behavior with me. The last time I heard from you was five days ago," Doris replied.

Harrison frowned. "Why did I think you'd be more logical than the average female? Sue me, Counselor, but I don't see the leap between what happened with us and you thinking I rushed from your bed to someone else's."

Doris snorted. "Oh, I am very logical. Did I track you down and demand a reckoning to make sure I was right? No, of course not. I have a life too, you know. And instead of waiting for a call that now I know was never coming, I called you... which every female in my family would have pointed out was the worst possible thing I should do in such a situation. Most forgotten females after sex like we had would have made a damn date with someone incredibly handsome and pretended not to give a damn that she never got a phone call. You're lucky I'm not one of those women."

Harrison winced, finally getting it. "Damn—okay. You're right. I should have called you to say hello or something. Everything just happened so fast this week. I made the house deal, then talked my father into going for some testing. Apparently they can shoot a balloon into your veins to let the blood flow better. It's scary, but I got him to agree to the procedure."

Still pondering her cold jealousy which was far worse than the haranguing tirades he'd experienced from other women, Harrison shot off down the course driving fast as Doris squealed beside him. He laughed but didn't slow down until they rolled up beside the first hole.

The vicious smack on his arm woke him right up to the fact she was still pissed.

"Stop this cart and let me the hell out of it. You drive like a maniac!" she yelled.

Harrison shrugged.

Climbing out of the cart, Doris walked to the back and pulled her line driver from the bag. "Just for that horrendous ride, I'm going first."

Harrison grinned as he watched her tee off. Her swing was sluggish. Her body was jerky and he noticed she seemed highly uncomfortable. That couldn't all be anger at him, could it?

"Are you taking meds or something?"

Doris watched her ball fall five feet short of the hole. "Damn it, you made me chop the shot." She turned and glared. "No, I'm not taking any meds."

"Smoking weed? You can tell me. I won't be offended. Everybody is doing a little pot these days."

Doris didn't answer. Instead, she lifted her driver like she intended to bash his head in with it. Maybe she did intend to.

Harrison took his time as he lined up his ball. "Well, if you're not using dope, then you must be royally pissed at me. So I'm sincerely sorry I didn't call you. Obviously I should have. I just got busy. That's really all it was."

Doris glared. "I can hear in your voice you still don't get how our fuck-a-thon might have had me a little confused. I really thought you sneaking out was your weasel way of saying goodbye. Your exit strategy was probably the one thing you failed to inform me about your previous encounters. Normally, when a guy disappears from my bed in the middle of the night, it's my cue to discreetly pay the concierge for his services the next morning. In this case, you didn't bother to leave a note about the bill. So I didn't know what the hell to think. A simple statement about needing to go to work would have helped clear things up."

His swing didn't even connect. It went right over his ball. "*Fuck-a-thon?* Is that what you thought happened between us?" He paused to look at her and knew it was the truth before she even made her case.

"Put yourself in my position, Harrison. Now add in a known womanizer that everyone and his cousin has decided I need to be warned about because I'm obviously too stupid to realize he preys on newly divorced women. Hell, my ex-husband even came to my office and warned me about you. Of course, he also wanted me to handle his divorce from the woman he got pregnant. See? I've had a busy five days too. Yet I still found freaking time to call and schedule this game. How about that for maturity?"

Harrison swung again and chopped the ball. It did a little skip hop and rolled three feet from the tee. He hung his head in shame of several kinds. Then he laughed.

"I'm sorry, Doris. I was just taking care of my father and making a sweet business deal. I was up early and home late and the days just… went by. When you called about playing golf, I thought it was your way of saying everything was still okay between us. I thought it meant you understood I'd gotten busy."

Doris frowned. He had a point, but she didn't like it. "I'm not a mind reader… and don't be ridiculous. Everything is okay between us. Take your shot. Quit fooling around."

Harrison lifted his head and stared. "You still don't sound okay."

"Because I'm not," Doris declared, glaring back. "I'm forty-three, pre-menopausal, and evidently have the worse case of PMS that I've ever had in my life. You fixed my bad mood for a single night, and then you never came back for a replay. I know it's not fair, but screw fair. I want to blame you for the way I feel so bad my teeth ache with it."

Harrison hung his head and laughed because he adored her honesty as much as the rest. "Then I'm sorry for that too. I see now I was only thinking of myself. Can I come take care of you tonight? I promise to make you forget your bad mood again."

Doris huffed. "Did our matching shirts wilt anything important?"

Harrison laughed loudly at her teasing. "No, ma'am. I've had a hard time coping these last few days myself, and yes, I mean that exactly like it sounds. I never knew that applied to women too. You've been a real education for me."

Doris looked back and saw another set of golfers approaching. "Great. Glad I could educate you. Now hit the damn ball, Harrison. I can't believe we're still playing the first hole."

Harrison chuckled as he lined up his shot again. "I'm not

touching that statement. No siree, baby. I'm way smarter than that."

He took a couple of practice swings, then sent the ball flying. It arced in the air and rolled smoothly into the first hole's cup for the first time ever since he'd been playing the course. Such stupid luck had to be an omen for him and Doris. The hole was so notoriously hard to score that he might have even tied some sort of record at the club for what he just did.

He grinned as he turned to the contrary woman he was falling for. She stared at his perfect shot with a demonic look of hatred. That cinched it. He was gaga in love with her.

"Show-off. Get in the damn cart," Doris ordered. "I'm driving this time."

Grinning over her continued grumbling, Harrison climbed into the passenger seat and clung to the dashboard as they shot off to the next flag like they were racing.

CHAPTER 12

Doris was humming in her kitchen as she made tea. Ruth was opening and shutting the door leading out to the patio.

"When did you get the door fixed?"

"Two days ago. Harrison fixed it for me," Doris said, dipping tea bags in their cups. "He took it off the hinges, shaved some wood off the bottom and top, and then put it back on. It's worked like a charm ever since. It took him ten minutes. I still can't believe it was so easy. All these years of it sticking… hell, I could have done that myself."

Ruth closed the door with a quiet click and came to perch at the counter. Doris met her sister's serene gaze and was happy to know she was supported.

"Talk to Mom and Dad lately?" Doris asked.

Ruth chuckled. "What did they do now?"

"Mom and Dad invited me to lunch last week so they could warn me off dating Harrison. I lasted a whole ten minutes. I delivered a scathing speech and left before the food came."

Ruth giggled. "You're not going to listen to their advice, are you?"

Doris laughed. "I wasn't really planning on it. Do you think I should?"

"Are you kidding me? You're glowing. Even if he leaves eventually, at least you've had a taste of what a good man is capable of making you feel."

"I'm not sure I can handle getting sex advice from my baby sister. Does Tim make you glow?" Doris asked, setting her sister's tea in front of her.

"If he did, I would just powder that shine away all day long. But if you're asking me if he's talented in bed... yes... very. It keeps getting better, and I don't know how that works. I'm just grateful."

Doris laughed and turned back to fetch her own tea. "Good to hear. I'm glad my sis is happy with her man."

Ruth picked up her tea and sipped. "Since we're swapping gossip, did you hear Avery is trying to divorce his baby's mother? Vivian said Freddie told her. His father's firm handles Avery's money."

"So much for the illusion of client privacy..." Doris mused, shaking her head.

"No. It's not like that," Ruth exclaimed. "It's that Avery made such a big deal about divorcing you and marrying her. Now his denial of his child has struck a chord in a lot of people. How can he keep saying the baby isn't his? He says he's going to make her take a paternity test to prove parentage."

Doris sighed heavily. "I know. He told me. He came to the office and asked me to handle his divorce."

Ruth hissed. "The nerve of him..."

Doris snorted. "Yes—but you know—I had the feeling there was something he wasn't revealing about the situation. There was a certain smirky sureness about him when he said it."

Ruth tilted her head. "Doris, really. No one can be that neutral about their ex. You got divorced when her condition started to show. Any reasonable woman would have taken that same action."

Doris smiled and waved her hand. "I don't know why we're talking about him. It's none of my business. I'm sleeping with a younger man who makes me glow."

"Braggart," Ruth declared, reaching over the bar to playfully smack her laughing sister's arm.

Doris snickered. "You'd think so, but it's not bragging if it's a fact."

～

HARRISON WATCHED his father's eyes flicker open. He smiled when recognition flared in their depths.

"Good. I'm not dead yet. Did it work?" Jefferson asked.

"Doctors seemed to think it did," Harrison replied. "They're going to be harping now on the smoking and drinking. If they make you choose your sins, I say keep the womanizing and shotgun the other vices from your life. That's what I would do."

Jefferson laughed. "You sound so much like Dad when you're joking around. I hope like hell you pass along those genes someday. If Grahams are remembered in Falls Church, I hope they think of you and Dad instead of me."

Harrison snorted. "I think I've temporarily shifted everyone's attention, though I confess my motivation was not on sparing your reputation."

Jefferson snorted back. "You talking about your recent tryst with the mannish Doris Pearson? God, Harrison—do you pick your affairs for their notoriety quotient? She's the biggest challenge you could have taken on."

Harrison rubbed the indention on the bridge of his nose. He'd started wearing his glasses to drive, but he hated the weight on his face the rest of the time. "I didn't realize you knew about my interest in Doris."

Jefferson waved his hand. "I have no right to talk about who you like. I know this."

"Dad," Harrison drew in a breath. "This is more than just *like*. I'm pretty sure I want to marry her."

Jefferson grabbed the bedrail with one hand and dragged the arm with the IV across his chest to hold himself while he laughed. "Don't tell me stuff like that. It hurts to laugh." He stopped when he saw his son's serious expression. "You *are* kidding, aren't you?"

"No, Dad. I'm not kidding. I'm falling in love with her," Harrison said quietly. "It wasn't anything I'd planned, but…"

"… you got caught in the Graham curse," Jefferson finished.

"Yes. Exactly," Harrison said, nodding. He was happy not to have to rationalize his attraction because he still didn't understand it. All he knew was that he wanted to be with Doris for the rest of his life.

Jefferson closed his eyes. "Then there's no use me trying to talk you out of it. She's old, though. If you're planning on children, you're going to have look around for a fling to have them. It will cost you some money, but you'd at least get a biological son or daughter out of it. Not the most optimal situation, but given how you've handled yourself with women up to now, I'd say you're clever enough to make it work."

"Dad… stop. I don't see that working out the way you're describing," Harrison said.

"No reason it shouldn't. Doris is savvy about such things. She stayed with Avery Vincent long enough to prove she can handle complex marital arrangements. I never did that to your mother because she would have left me over another child. Wait… strike all that. Doris left Avery over a baby. What was I thinking? Must be the meds. You'll have to keep your love child a secret."

Harrison rubbed a hand over his face. Doris was more apt to castrate him than tolerate any wandering—not that he wanted to wander. She was all the challenge he needed in bed or out.

Children would have been nice to have at some point. Maybe down the line they could do something to get one. He couldn't think of such obstacles now. All he wanted at the moment was to talk her into letting him wake up beside her each day so Doris would know he'd always be coming home to her at the end of it.

His past—and hers—would be erased more quickly if they were around each other enough to build some real trust. He knew he had a bit of philandering to socially live down. Luckily, Doris didn't seem put off by people talking about them.

He wasn't intimidated by what it would take to work things out with Doris because he knew what he wanted. He wanted coffee on the patio and to talk with Doris about stocks over breakfast. He wanted to fix things and make her smile like she had about the patio door. She was still praising him for that one.

And he for damn sure wanted to help her find some women's golf clothes that let her move like she wanted, but didn't look like his. Her dressing like a man bothered him because he knew it was one of the many things people used as excuses to talk about her behind her back. That's why his father had called her "mannish".

Of course, if the male gossipers had known the kind of lover Doris was in bed, they would have done their damndest to cut him up the back. He was no fool.

For the first time in his life, he honestly wanted to get married, and not just because it was a good idea. He wanted a wife only because marrying Doris increased his chances of keeping her forever. He didn't want any other woman. There were no substitutes.

"… none of that surprised me, though. I knew the baby probably wasn't his," Jefferson said.

"What?" Harrison pulled his wandering thoughts back to his father. "Sorry, Dad. I missed what you said."

"I was talking about Avery Vincent planning to divorce his new wife. When Doris finds out she's going to kill him for lying to her all those years. I knew he wasn't the kid's father when I first heard about the baby. Avery married Celeste Stanton thinking to replace the money he didn't get out of Doris in the divorce. Rumor is that he talked Celeste into having a threesome. Whoever the kid was that joined them for their sex party—he's the baby's biological father. Her parents hate Avery. It wouldn't surprise me to hear Vincent planned to get Celeste knocked up so he could legitimately marry her."

"You sound pretty sure about Avery's lack of parentage given it's just hearsay," Harrison declared, sitting up straighter.

Jefferson snorted. "I'm not the only one sure. The first decade they were married, Doris had every test known to man done and doctors could find absolutely nothing wrong with her. Caroline Pearson—the woman you swear is chair of the gossip committee —still talks about her *poor barren daughter.*"

"Maybe all that is simply a mother worrying about her eldest child."

Jefferson rolled his eyes. "This isn't gossip, son. What most people don't know is that Avery had the mumps when he was a kid. They dropped to his testicles and made him sterile. I know this because he dated Angela before I married her. She said Avery used that as his reason for not wanting to use a rubber."

Harrison ran a hand over his hair. He was secretly grossed out by the idea of Doris's ex-husband having had sex with his current stepmother. His father following up Vincent was bad enough to imagine, but it was like he'd suddenly turned into a prude where Doris was concerned. He wanted to shield her from all that stuff. He wanted to make love to her and only her, until they really were as close as his grandparents had been.

"Maybe Angela was exaggerating. Maybe she told you that stuff to make you jealous."

Jefferson laughed softly. "That's charitable of you, son. Everyone knows Avery pays dearly from his trust fund to indulge his darker tastes. An unplanned baby would have messed things up permanently with Doris, and he would never have taken that risk because she paid for his cushy life. So if Vincent isn't into using rubbers with women who could conceive, he's not worried about making any babies. Didn't you use protection with all your women to keep stuff from happening?"

Harrison shrugged, now completely uncomfortable with the discussion. "Of course... I didn't want an accident. I also stayed away from eager young girls who might have had ambitious intentions."

Jefferson held up a tired finger. "Because you are a smart man and I raised you right in at least that one area. Kinky men who fool around should be a lot more responsible than Vincent."

"Damn it, Dad. Now you got me wondering what kind of shit Avery Vincent talked Doris into doing while they were married. Can we drop this conversation?"

Jefferson laughed. "Sorry. I probably shouldn't have said anything. I'm just happy to be alive and that I haven't done anything so horrendous that you hate my guts. If it helps, Doris doesn't come across to *anyone* as the kind of woman to let herself be taken advantage of in most ways. I hear she's hell on opposing attorneys in court. Judges love her. She's a no bullshit kind of person across the board. I can see why you'd not be put off by that trait. You're just like that too."

"No. I'm not put off. I like nearly everything about her. And thanks for the compliment."

"Well, you're smart financially too. Doris has family wealth and her own money. Marrying her would be a great investment in the future. It never hurts to have a wealthy wife. Leave it to you to find a smart one as well. If she'd had bigger breasts, I might have paid more attention myself."

"Geez, Dad." Harrison glared at his sleazy father. "Eyes off, old man. I found her first."

Harrison's mind stumbled after his father laughed. What if his father's stories were true about Avery?

He and Doris certainly hadn't been careful with each other. Nothing unusual had happened so far... not that he would have cared if he'd gotten her pregnant... but Doris might care. Her life would be the one most affected. If Avery had lied and he'd shunned being careful... wow, the real truth could be a shocker to them all.

It made him shudder to think of the wonderfully sexual woman he'd slept with trying to please someone as perverted as Avery Vincent. If the man's twisted urges were true, no wonder Doris had moved into a separate bedroom. She was loving and generous and very responsive. His other sexual experiences had paled and faded into nothing more important than high school groping.

"I was teasing, son. I'd never go after your girlfriend. Bring Doris around when you get the chance. I promise not to hit on her."

Harrison snickered and mock-glared at his ill father. "Angela and I would both kill you. We wouldn't wait for your heart to give out."

Jefferson chuckled as he moved restlessly against the sheets—the meds catching up to him again. "Thanks for making me laugh, Harrison. You always did have the ability to make my day. Helping create you was the best thing I ever did in my life. God bless your mother. She was a good woman."

Harrison didn't answer. Instead, he brooded as he watched his father fall back into his medicated sleep. Growing up with his father constantly embarrassing his mother with his skirt chasing, he'd gotten pretty hardened to gossip. That had naturally carried over to what people thought about him. Before Doris, he'd never cared one whit about the stories floating around. Now, he had a starring role and the last thing he wanted was to create more controversy for her.

Harrison leaned back in the chair and crossed his arms, his

mind going to the possibility of a pregnant Doris instead of a pre-menopausal, pre-menstrual cycle, hormonally horny one.

Would he even be able to tell the difference? Probably not, but he didn't care either way so long as he kept getting to share her bed.

CHAPTER 13

Today was one of those days Doris wished she'd stayed in bed. Her periods over the last six months were either a week long bloodbath or a couple days of nearly nothing. It was like having no menses at all. Normally, she groused through them either way because like all females, she'd learned not to let her cycle control her life.

This month's torture time was gearing up to be a doozie. So tired she couldn't see straight, even after getting a solid eight last night, she was fighting not to lay her head down on her desk. Tiredness fled to be replaced by a headache when Karen walked into her office unannounced and closed the door behind her. All she could think was... *shit—not again.*

Sighing in resignation over the woman's wide-eyed stare, Doris shook her head, surprised at the dizziness the action caused. The dizziness was a new twist to the hormonal craziness her doctor had been helping her cope with... and it wasn't fun to deal with. She might also have to get her blood sugar checked if this kept up.

"I'm sorry to barge in, Doris," Karen said in apology, wringing her hands. "But I couldn't call about this over the intercom. I'm even having trouble believing it's happening. This is bad… very, very bad."

Doris's eyebrows rose at the second "very" before she chuckled. "I'm having déjà vu, Karen. What's going on now? Avery come back?"

Karen put her hand on her chest and drew in a breath. "No, your ex-husband isn't here, but his new wife is, and she's insisting on talking to you. She said if you didn't agree to talk to her, she was going to talk to a newspaper reporter instead and make sure she mentioned your gossiping, self-righteous parents in her interview. That was her description, Doris—not mine. Sorry."

Doris removed her readers and tossed them on the desk in front of her. "Using blackmail to see me? That's a new one. Even my worst clients don't go that far."

Karen shrugged. "The woman kept escalating her argument, and I admit I finally ran out of patience. I refused to let her see you because she wouldn't tell me what she wanted. She said it was none of my business. Can you imagine someone being so rude?"

Doris covered her mouth to stifle her laugh. Though still miffed about the woman's guerrilla tactics, she admired the way Celeste Stanton Vincent had outmaneuvered Karen. That was no small feat, and she could see why her frazzled office manager had needed the extra adverb to explain her feelings.

"Well, don't worry, Karen. I'm sure you did your best. Send her back and let's see what she thinks is so important. Buzz me with a ten-minute warning before my nine o'clock is due."

"I will," Karen said firmly before heading back out the door.

She returned two minutes later and ushered a very pregnant woman into her office. Celeste politely thanked Karen before finally looking in her direction. After the door had shut completely, she waddled over to a chair and eased herself down into it, not really making direct eye contact.

Doris forced out a greeting. She wanted to establish the territory for their meeting was hers. "Hello, Mrs. Vincent. I only have a short time before my first appointment. What can I do for you?"

"I imagine I'm the last person you want to see, but there's something private I have to ask you. Before I ask my question, though, you need to understand this is not about me. This is about my baby. That's the only reason I would ever show up here."

"All right." Doris put her hands on top of her desk and let fingertips touch as she leaned forward. It was something judges did that was always extremely intimidating. The woman shifted in her chair. "I admit I'm curious about what would cause you to blackmail my office manager to get in to see me. That's mostly why I had her send you back instead of calling security to escort you out."

"I swear I'm not here to cause you any trouble—no real trouble anyway. This is not easy for me, but becoming a mother has changed things. Or rather Avery's defection has changed my mind about him."

The woman shifted multiple times, obviously not comfortable in the small, stiff chair. Doris felt the chink in her emotional armor happen, but couldn't stop it. Her normal shields were suddenly nowhere to be found. This is what being tired always did to her.

"What can I do for you?" Doris asked softly, wanting to get to the point so she could get this meeting over with quickly.

The woman used all the strength she had to pull herself as upright as possible in her seat. Doris sighed as she watched, finally feeling sorry for the woman carrying her ex-husband's child. She hated when the empathy thing got in the way of her own self-preservation. It was a little known weakness in her character which she meticulously hid from everyone.

"Avery says he's sure our baby's not his. He says he can't even get a woman pregnant. I can't trust anything he says right now, but I figured you would know the truth. All I'm asking is if you'll tell me if he's lying. I need to know so I can make… other plans."

"Oh," Doris said, consigning Avery to hell. He was a complete bastard to torment the mother of his child. "When no children happened for us, Avery and I were both medically checked. This happened early in our marriage. Neither of us seemed to have any medical problems that were preventing conception, but no children came either. All I can do is report my own experience. I really can't answer your question definitively."

The woman nodded and swallowed. Then Doris watched Celeste's expression shift from sadness to anger.

"So you're saying Avery *could* be the father, then?"

"No. I'm saying I was told Avery had no medical problems. If there is any question in *your* mind, I think the only way you're going to get more information about your child's father is to have a paternity test done. The tests can be up to ninety-nine percent accurate in ruling out Avery as a possibility… or vice versa. However, it is a very expensive test for results that still have a wide margin of error. Most women tend to be able to narrow parentage down well enough without it."

"Unless they need to know completely for sure because there is a dowry and a trust fund involved. My parents are being hard-nosed about this." Celeste sighed as she frowned. "Despite what people think, I'm a monogamous woman, Ms. Pearson. I think of myself only as an adventurous one. Avery made certain there was another man present the night I conceived. He said he wanted to watch and that any baby we created would still be his no matter what we did. All three of us were completely involved in creating this life I carry. That will always be my opinion of what happened."

"Which is more information than I wanted or needed to know about your situation since I have zero interest in your sex life with my ex-husband," Doris exclaimed sharply, waving a hand. "Look—I don't normally give unsolicited advice, but I highly suggest you not tell anyone else that story until it's a matter of life or death. I'm used to hearing such things, but you will be judged harshly if that story gets around the club."

"Didn't Avery ever ask to watch you be with someone else?"

Doris wanted to be righteously angry over the question and say no simply to keep her private life private, but decided she'd be better served to let gossips think she was a prude. And there would be gossip. There was always gossip in Falls Church, especially among families like the new Mrs. Vincent's. Before the week was out, Doris knew everyone in town would know about Celeste's visit.

"Okay… only between us… I turned Avery down when he asked me to let a stranger into our bed. I don't think it's a secret he got his kinky needs met elsewhere and as often as possible. Some will call me a prude for refusing my husband anything, but frankly I'm not into sharing myself with two men."

"To each his own," Celeste said, shrugging a shoulder. "The guy he brought to me was very good-looking so I said okay. I'm sexually open-minded. Avery asked to marry me the moment we found out about the baby, even before your divorce from him had happened. He was very kind and supportive for the first few months, so I wasn't worried. Then my parents got involved."

Doris nodded. "Yes. Parents tend to do that."

"My mother caught Avery flirting with another woman at the club the night of the dance. That's why she and my father decided they were going to make me wait for my trust fund money until I was thirty. That's a whole six years away, Ms. Pearson. Now that my trust fund isn't happening, Avery suddenly doesn't want the baby or me. What am I supposed to think about his motives?"

Doris lifted both hands. "I don't know. I divorced Avery so he could marry you and legally claim the child you carry. I'm afraid that's as far as I'm willing to be involved. All other situations between you and Avery are yours to work out. "

Celeste nodded. She pushed herself out of the chair. "I guess in your place, I'd be screaming at me to leave after what I just told you. Thanks for talking to me, Ms. Pearson. I think I'm going to skip the paternity test. Avery originally said he wanted the baby, and I'm going to hold him to his word. I don't think I'm going to be able to forgive him for what he's done to my reputation and I guess I'll have to live down being married to him just like you did. I'm sorry for fooling around with him before you divorced him."

Doris stared and blinked, stunned by the younger woman's apology, which didn't match her total lack of true remorse. Young people. Was she really that far out of touch?

"Don't waste any guilt on me, Celeste. My life is better now than it's been in years, and I have found that reputations are mostly mythical. All a person can really do is hold their head high and live life on their own terms. I wish you and your child the best of luck."

Celeste Vincent slowly turned and walked to the door, stopping mid-walk to turn back. "Thanks again for seeing me. I hope you find someone wonderful who appreciates you. Everyone deserves that."

"Yes, they do. And I'm sure your parents will eventually support you regardless of Avery. Babies have a way of bringing peace to troubled families. I hope that becomes the truth in your case."

Doris watched Avery's new wife walk to her office door and ease through it. Why wasn't she feeling some strong emotion about their discussion—like rage or at least disgust? Instead, she merely felt extremely sorry for the woman and even more regretful about ever having married a man like Avery Vincent in the first place. She'd seen a lot of sad things in her work, but personally knowing a woman her ex-husband had tricked into getting pregnant now topped the list.

If she had not gone back to Avery after their horrible wedding night, she might have had a very different sort of life. Yet the life she'd led was a life that had recently allowed her to let someone like Harrison Graham into it… however briefly he ended up staying.

Without Avery and her parents, instead of being a lawyer, she might have become a pro golfer. That had certainly been on her mind in college. As a women's golf pro, she probably would have married some club swinging athlete who had no idea how to fix a stuck patio door.

Would her pro boyfriend have given her two or three orgasms when he spent the night the way Harrison could? Since the orgasms Harrison gave her usually resulted in blissful sleep and contentment, she was just going to appreciate the present and not worry about her past. It couldn't be changed anyway.

Not wanting to dwell on Avery and Celeste's sordid lifestyle, or the negative effect of it on a child that wasn't yet born, Doris gave in to the tiredness she was feeling and laid her head down on her desk. She dropped instantly into an exhausted sleep.

She was startled awake twenty-five minutes later when the intercom buzzer announced her first real appointment of the day.

CHAPTER 14

"Let your heel come up more on the follow-through," Doris commanded.

Harrison felt Doris's body brush the entire back of his as she stepped behind him to illustrate her point physically. His mind was on everything but his golf swing as she swept a hand over his right hip. It ran down to just behind his knee, and she used her impressive strength to bend his leg until he was all but standing on the toe of his shoe.

Harrison chuckled at her manhandling. "Are we playing golf or doing ballet?"

"Call it what you want, but I want you to go up on that toe during your swing through. Play another ball and practice it, laughing boy. The next golfers are still two holes behind us."

"Fine," Harrison grumbled, missing her heat when she stepped away from him. "You're sure being a hard-ass this morning. For a moment there, I thought I'd joined the military."

Doris snickered as she stepped out of range. She pointed to the tee. "Take your shot and do what I told you. This is a very important lesson."

Harrison stepped backward and took a couple swings to

practice his golf swing ballet move before he stepped forward again. He lined up his shot, drew his club back in an arc, then heard the click of connection at the very same moment he heard the swish of wind off his club.

They both watched his solidly hit ball sail through the air, bounce once, and then roll less than a foot from the ninth hole.

"I'll be damned," he exclaimed.

"See? That was wonderful… except you forgot to yell out your swing. I know you don't normally have to worry about such things."

"Hey now," Harrison grumbled.

"If anyone had been ahead of us, you might have taken their head off with the power behind that well-played ball."

When he turned to glare at her for chastising him instead of celebrating his success, Doris burst out laughing. He snorted, then smiled at his talented tormentor. "That better not be innuendo out here in the open. I didn't say a damn thing when you copped a feel of my ass."

"I will neither confirm nor deny said attempt to cop something of yours during my demonstration," Doris declared.

Harrison barely fought the urge to adjust himself. The woman could rev his engine with nothing but words. "You have me all confused. I don't know whether to thank you or spank you."

"Interesting way of showing your gratitude," Doris said as she dug for a ball. "Are you offering me a choice?"

Harrison grinned and carried his club back to his bag. "No. You're just going to say you want both. I know that by now."

"True… I do like your hands on me," Doris said, giggling over her daring reply as she chose a club. She bent to set the tee again and put her ball on it. When she straightened, a wave of dizziness swept over her. "Whoa. I am really going to have to get a check-up soon. That's like the third time in two weeks that I've gotten dizzy. I can't believe my body is falling apart at forty-three. What the hell is going on? I keep in good shape."

Harrison reached her in her three strides and gripped her arm. "Why are you getting dizzy?"

Doris laughed up into his concerned face. She couldn't seem to help herself... or take his worry seriously. "Blood sugar? Blood pressure? I don't know. Maybe it's stress. First, Avery came to see me, and then a few days ago Celeste stopped by."

Harrison gripped harder. "Why the hell didn't you tell me Avery's new wife came to see you?"

Doris snorted. "Because it was a private conversation between me and her at my place of business. It's not like I invited her to dinner at my house. All the woman did was ask me a couple questions and apologize. No one dies from being made uncomfortable, Harrison. Trust me, I know. As an attorney, I make people uncomfortable all the time—on purpose."

"Well, what did she apologize to you for? It should have been for sleeping with your damn husband," Harrison said sharply. If the woman hadn't slept with Avery, Doris still might be legally bound to him. His mind couldn't even go there now. He considered her his already.

"I'm still not sure what Celeste was trying to accomplish," Doris answered. "Why does me talking to her bother you so much? She wasn't any more saintly or guilty than any of the rest my clients... or me, for that matter. I'm well used to dealing with the scandalous and the inappropriate."

Harrison let go of her arm. "It doesn't make me uncomfortable," he finally ground out, wishing that were the case, but it wasn't. He was lying. "I just don't see why those two have to keep coming around you. You divorced Avery... and Celeste coming to see you is just... tacky."

"Tacky?" Doris exclaimed, laughing at the term as she pushed Harrison away from her. "Move back. They're catching up to us." She lined up, yelled "fore", and sent the ball sailing. It bounced and rolled until it stopped right beside Harrison's.

"Damn show-off," he said, grinning when she started giggling again. "You and your ballerina moves. Just for that, I'm driving the cart for the rest of the game."

Doris grimaced. "Okay. But I'm still not feeling great. If you go too fast, I may barf all over you and your fancy golf clothes."

Harrison huffed. "I wouldn't have to dress so fancy if you'd stop wearing shirts that match mine. This is the stuff I usually save for when I play with well-heeled clients. Because of you, I now carry spare clothing in the trunk of my car in case we're wearing the same color."

"You're so fashion conscious. At least your golf swing is grateful for my comfortable clothes, even if you aren't." Doris rolled her eyes as she climbed into the cart beside her grinning boyfriend.

She squealed when Harrison tramped down on the gas feed as hard as possible and the cart shot forward. The man was laughing at her discomfort the whole time.

WITH A LIGHT CASELOAD for the day, she was able to take an opening that afternoon with her regular physician. She was putting her clothes back on when a nurse stuck her head back into the examination room. The woman held out a plastic cup complete with lid.

"Sorry, Doris. Dr. Benson wants to do one more test," she said cheerily. "All we need you to do is capture a urine sample in this cup. There are clean catch directions in the bathroom, along with wipes and anything else you might need."

"Are you testing for diabetes?" Doris asked, her voice revealing her alarm.

The nurse winced and made a face. "I'm really not allowed to say what we're testing for, but I can tell you that this is all very routine. Dr. Benson is probably trying to rule out things. Just slide the cup through the little window in the bathroom when you're done. We'll see it and take it to the lab for testing. You can wait in here for him."

Doris nodded and headed to the bathroom with her specimen cup. With the task completed, she washed up and finished righting her skirt and blouse. She pulled her cardigan back on too because she had gotten a chill sitting in the air conditioned examination room.

Half an hour later, she had read all the provided magazines, and everything on the walls. Now, she was pacing restlessly. Two sharp raps on the door heralded her doctor's return. John had the strangest look on his face she'd ever seen him have.

"Good Lord, John. The expression on your face is terrifying. Am I dying?"

Her doctor of nearly two decades shook his head and kept the serious look on his face as he spoke softly.

"No. You are in remarkable health except for one tiny thing growing inside your body. Right now, it's probably the size of your little fingernail."

Doris held up her hand and examined her smallest fingernail. "I see. Is it operable?" She got a little mad when her favorite doctor laughed at her question.

"Sure. It's operable… if that's how you want to handle things. We'll schedule surgery for about seven months from now."

Doris sank down into a nearby chair. "Oh God… I have cancer, don't I?"

"*Cancer?* No. Of course not," John denied hotly, shaking his head. "Have you had intimate relations with Avery in the last few months?"

"Why? Did my sleazy ex-husband give me a damn disease? He did, didn't he?" Doris rose to her full towering height. "I'll kill him. First, I'll sue him for… *something*… I don't know. I'll take everything he has and then I'll kill him. I want to watch him die. I'll enjoy every blessed minute of Avery taking his last damn breath—the sleazy bastard."

She backed up when John stood and held her gaze. "Doris… please. Calm yourself. You're an older woman and this kind of agitation is not healthy for someone in your condition. We need to talk about what I found very calmly and rationally."

"And that's another thing… I hate my age being pointed out to me every five minutes. A woman turns forty and suddenly life is over for her," Doris complained, sitting again. "How about you skip the pep talk and simply tell me the worst of it, John? My mind is creating bad scenarios faster than you can talk about your findings."

"Okay. First… medical tests don't always tell us everything. For example, apparently Avery can father a child after all."

Doris stared in disbelief. Where had that random reference come from? "Well, of course he can, John. Celeste Vincent is about to deliver their child any day now."

"Yes, that's right, but…"

Doris shook her head. "I will admit that I've seen Avery more lately than I did the last five years we were living in the same house. But what has that got to do with anything?"

John sighed, resigned to being the bad messenger. "Well, Avery's visits are precisely why I'm the bearer of such surprising news today. Your attempt to reconcile has resulted in a little something you probably weren't planning on happening."

Doris shook her head and frowned. "Reconcile? What are you insinuating, John? I… *damn it*… I wish people would stay the hell out of my personal business. I'm dating another man, okay, John? I'm dating someone new. That's not a crime, even in stuffy Falls Church."

"Oh… *there's someone new*," John said, rubbing his chin. "Well, that's interesting, and maybe explains things better."

"*Things?* Is that a medical term?" Doris let out a long frustrated breath. "How many times do I have to say this to people? My love life—or lack of one—is no one's business."

Doris only backed down her tone when John held up a hand to stop her from lecturing him.

"In this one case, your love life is my business. Okay, here goes with the bluntness I probably should have led with. Doris Isette Pearson... I'm not a hundred percent sure, but I am mostly certain that you're pregnant."

The news was like being slapped in the face. Only there was no pain. The shock of it was all she felt.

Doris shook her head. "No. I can't be pregnant. That's... that's... *impossible.*"

John shook his head just as firmly. "No. We never medically determined that. In fact, we never found anything wrong with you at all. Babies just never came, so it was easy to assume you weren't equipped to have them. That was a wrong assumption."

"But I'm old now. You just said so. You called me an *older woman.* I heard you," Doris exclaimed.

"Unplanned pregnancies happen more often to women in their forties than most people realize. Fluctuating hormones as a woman starts the decade before menopause can result in an optimal time for pregnancy to occur. Have you been using any birth control with the new man in your life?"

"No, because he was a mostly decent guy and I knew I couldn't get pregnant. You said you aren't completely sure, John. Maybe you're wrong about this. Maybe it's some sort of false reading. There could be all kinds of explanations. Right?"

John sat on the rolling stool in the exam room and calmly stared into his patient's stunned gaze. "Yes. It's possible I'm wrong. Labs still can't differentiate between hCG and a lutenizing hormone which makes the urine test not one hundred percent. However, combined with your reported symptoms of heightened sensitivity to smell, mood swings, and dizziness, the evidence makes the odds of this being a real pregnancy pretty high, Counselor. Care to refute your other symptoms?"

"*Oh, Lord,*" Doris said, putting a hand on her stomach.

Something was now growing in there. "How can I be a mother at my age? I don't know anything about taking care of an infant."

She groaned when John rolled forward and gently took both her hands in his.

"No. Don't look at me like that, John. I don't want the concerned physician lecture. Can't you simply tell me I was dumb to take chances and that the tests aren't true? I promise I'll be more careful in the future."

She felt like an idiot. All those orgasms and she'd never once considered the virility of the man who gave them to her. Now she panicked when the one man who knew nearly as much about her body as Harrison did cleared his throat and took a deep breath.

"If you truly never gave conceiving a child with your new man any thought, then I can only imagine your level of shock at hearing this news. I don't give out many referrals to take care of this situation without going to term, but I would certainly do that for you, Doris. You don't have to become a mother at this age if you don't want to become one. You'll have to travel to have the procedure done, but I can give you all the referrals you need to do it safely."

She might be in shock, but Doris still knew her own mind about such things. That option was not on her list of solutions to her dilemma. Shaking her head made her dizzy again. She had to stop in order to speak.

"No. I would never get rid of any child... especially not his." She couldn't say Harrison's name until he knew. "Oh God, this is just such a surprise. I'm not even prepared to *think* about it as reality. I care about the man I'm dating, but I never saw this happening to us."

John nodded and squeezed both her hands. "I highly suggest you talk to the biological father before making any permanent decision, but don't wait too long. Based on our brief look at the your menses calendar, you're in the middle of your second month. Are you on good terms with the father?"

"The biological father? Yes. We're on good terms. I mean…
we're still seeing each other."

Doris swallowed when she heard John chuckle over her verbal
stumbling.

Harrison. John didn't know they were talking about Harrison
Graham.

Oh Lord… Harrison Graham was the father of her child. He
might think she'd done this on purpose. Everyone else would.

Groaning as reality hit, Doris hung her head at the very idea of
all the gossip her condition was going to inspire. John patting her
shoulder brought her attention back to what he was saying.

"I know this is quite the shock after all these years of believing
you couldn't conceive. Do you need me to call someone for you?"

"Yes," Doris said meekly, needing to tell the only other
sympathetic person she had in her life. "Call Ruth and ask her to
come get me. Please don't tell her what's wrong. I'll do that."

"Okay. You want me to call your mother too?" John asked.

"No." Doris snorted at the very idea, but it wasn't really funny.
Her parents were going to disown her for good now. "My mother
wanted me to buy off Avery's new wife so I could keep my
cheating ex-husband. Pearson women must keep up appearances,
you know."

John sighed as he shook his head. "How many years have I
known you, Doris? I'm going to be honest here. Divorcing was the
smartest thing you've ever done for yourself. Want me to talk to
Caroline and Dennis for you? I'll do my best to set them straight."

"No—I'll handle my parents. But thank you, John. I never
realized there were so many good men running around in the
world."

Doris stunned both of them by throwing her arms around him
and hugging tightly.

John patted and sighed. "Doris, remember those early
menopausal hormone surges we talked about? Baby ones are just
as strong. You're going to want reduce your stress as much as

possible. This would be a good time for you to play some more golf."

Doris raised her head and stared before giving in to her urge to laugh hysterically.

~

RUTH'S HANDS on the steering wheel were slick with sweat from worry. "Talk to me, Doris. John looked so serious when he walked you out to my car. I'm so scared I can barely drive."

"I'm going to tell you everything. Take me home first. If you can stick around until I come to my senses, I'll probably need a ride back to collect my car."

"Maybe Harrison can take you."

"No," Doris answered, shaking her head. "Not tonight. I can't talk to him yet. I need time to think about this first."

Ruth firmed her lips and nodded. They completed the rest of the drive in silence.

Once in the house, Doris walked to the patio door and went outside into the afternoon sun. She stood in the full sunlight beyond her arbor and looked out at the wild and wooly English garden she loved so much.

If John was right about her being nearly two months along, that meant she must have conceived the first night she spent with Harrison. Oh My God... she could actually pinpoint her child's conception to the exact day it happened. How many women could say that?

Doris hung her head remembering that night. It had been as close to magic as she'd ever experienced. Tears leaked from her eyes thinking about a baby coming from all that heat and passion. She wondered if Harrison was going to feel the same way when he found out.

She didn't know how long she stood there thinking. When she

raised her head, Ruth was standing silently by her side, looking solemn, yet simply waiting on her to collect herself.

Her sister's thoughtfulness meant the world to her in that moment.

"I'm sorry if I scared you. I'm not dying," Doris said at last. "I'm… oh lord, I can't believe I'm saying this at my age. Ruth… God, Ruth… John is pretty sure I'm pregnant. How crazy is that?"

Ruth drew in a stunned breath, clapped her hands, and then burst into relieved tears. "Oh, honey…" She threw her arms around her sister and hugged tight. "That's so wonderful. And Harrison's the father. Your child is going to be so smart. I'm so happy for you both."

"*Smart?* Ruth, didn't you hear me? Harrison Graham got me pregnant because I did nothing to stop it from happening. Everyone we know is going to think I did this to him on purpose. The gossip committee at the club is going to say I trapped the man into being a permanent part of my life. People are going to think I'm… you know… one of *those* women."

"Like you ever cared what people at the club thought about you." Ruth laughed at the statement, stepped away, and wiped her eyes with both hands. "Give me a minute here. I thought I was losing you forever. My mind has to adjust to the news being much less worse than I thought."

Doris blew out a breath. "I'm sorry. I truly didn't mean to scare you. I'm just shocked."

"Not half as much as Mom and Dad are going to be," Ruth teased, fighting a smile. "That should at least stop Mom's wagging tongue for a while. She'll be too busy finding a way to spin this situation in a good light."

Doris sighed and stared out into the garden again. She still hadn't cleaned her green dress. She'd hung it back in the closet, grass stains and all. The stained dress was now a souvenir of the best night of her life. She had yet to let the man responsible know how much his extraordinary lovemaking had meant to her.

"I can barely tell Harrison I like him. How am I going to tell him about the baby?"

Ruth giggled. "You say… *Harrison, I'm pregnant. The baby is yours.*"

Doris gave her a sour look. "Because it's so easy to do that to a man you never intended to keep. He'll be as stunned as I am. No one expects it to happen to someone my age."

Ruth grinned and nodded. "Well… you still don't have to keep the man… but you do have to tell him about the baby. Harrison's going to figure it out anyway when you start showing."

Doris nodded. "I know, but I just can't stop wondering. Why didn't this happen before? I never used anything with Avery… ever… not even when he kept fooling around. Initially, I wasn't worried about diseases and so on. After a while I got smarter. When he refused to wear protection, I started to refuse all his advances. But I also never used protection with any other man I slept with."

"You've slept with men other than Avery and Harrison?" Ruth asked in surprise.

Doris winced. The truth had just slipped out. "Yes. Those trips to Europe… I was trying to become the woman my husband seemed to need. I rented them."

"Oh, Doris. What a life that horrible husband of yours drove you to. That's not how a mutually satisfying sex life works. It's the 60s. A woman needs to exert her right to her own pleasure. You should read Dr. Helen Kaplan's research into sexuality. She's totally right about female orgasm."

Doris shoulders sagged even as they shook with laughter. Her sister had used her college degree and her intelligence in some unusual ways. "I assumed my sex education needed to be done physically, so that's how I approached it. I had good intentions, but the bottom line is I didn't honor my marriage vows any more than Avery did. I'm surprised you're not disappointed in me."

Ruth slipped an arm around her sister's waist. "Stop that. You were trying to survive a terrible husband. And obviously that training made you talented enough to keep a man like Harrison coming back for more."

"Ruth, I'm ten years older than Harrison. His infatuation with me will die with every new line I get on my face. I see it every day at work. A man hits forty or forty-five and dumps his wife of twenty years for a twenty-year-old with perky breasts. I'd be a fool to set myself up for that."

Ruth shrugged. "I wouldn't rule out anything, Doris. Harrison Graham doesn't seem to be like most men. And you're going to be gaining a lot of weight shortly. That will keep the lines smoothed out for months… maybe even a year or two if you're slow at losing the baby weight. No one will know how old you are for a good long time yet."

Doris laughed. Baby weight. Another foreign concept to her. "Thanks for coming after me. I love you, Ruth."

"I love you too. Now let's go back inside. I'm going to make you some tea… herbal of course. You're going to need to give up the caffeine for a while. Then when we're done with our tea, we'll go back and get your car. This is not the end of the world. This is the beginning of your biggest adventure. Let's look at it that way."

Doris sighed about all the changes coming to life and let her sister lead her back inside.

CHAPTER 15

A KNOCK ON HER OFFICE DOOR HAD HER SAGGING HEAD POPPING UP reluctantly. Every morning this week she had been tired and sluggish. In the evenings, her energy perked up, but that wasn't helping her court cases being tried during the day. Clients had a tendency to book morning appointments and thought it was perfectly normal to meet before nine o'clock.

"Come in," she called to the still closed door.

Karen opened it and carried a manila envelope across the room to her. "This just arrived by messenger. I signed for proof of service, but I don't think this is for one of your cases. I think it's for you personally."

Her head spun as she took the package. Dizziness was evidently her new best friend. Man, she needed some extra sleep. "Thanks, Karen. I'll take a look at it in a little bit."

"Okay. I'm going to make you some tea with honey. You look like you need a boost this morning."

"Thank you, Karen. That would be very nice," Doris replied, her eyes on the envelope.

As her office manager disappeared, she slipped the official documents out of it. On top was a letter addressed to her. Behind that was a copy of what appeared to be the country club's bylaws. She thumbed through the pages noting several were tagged with paper clips.

Wondering what was going on, she read the letter closely. Her disbelief grew with every line.

She set the letter aside and hit the intercom. "Karen, I'm going to have a rush litigation I need drafted as soon as you're free to help me."

"Of course. Should I arrange for a courier this afternoon?"

"No," Doris said firmly. "I'll do the serving myself. Can we get it done by eleven-thirty? It won't take me long to draw it up."

"I think that's possible. Are you okay, Doris?"

"Yes… but I wish I had normal parents instead of the ones I have," Doris replied dryly.

She stared at the letter as she thought about what to do. It was mostly a scare tactic and they should have known better than to challenge her that way. Mixed gender golf games were not against the rules. She and Harrison had violated no bylaws by her training him.

Insinuating her parents were in full support of the club's "corrective measures" was bad enough. Threatening to take Lloyd's job and put sanctions on Ruth's family was not.

It was time to stop letting people at the country club think they could judge her without suffering the consequences of their narrow minds.

HOW DID anyone ever put their pasts behind them enough to have a present? His dating history seemed determined to not stay history. For the first time in his life, Harrison was feeling sincere regret for his actions. He should have never dated women at the country club.

He leaned across the table, staring down the woman who'd

drafted the letter he'd gotten from the club's ethics committee. He'd bet Doris had gotten one too. He was also pretty sure it was his fault the warning had been issued. Ginny Wilson seemed to be holding a grudge over bad behavior he'd all but forgotten.

"Mixed gender games aren't expressly forbidden and neither are golf lessons. If the club sent the same letter to Doris, she's going to be embarrassed for about five seconds, and then she's going to get really mad. Making a long-standing club member— and an outstanding attorney—mad doesn't seem like very smart business, Ginny."

"Golf lessons, huh? Is that what you're calling your liaison with the woman who couldn't keep her own husband happy in bed?"

Harrison sighed. "Look, Ginny, I'm sorry I behaved so poorly with you. I know we didn't part on the best of terms."

"What kind of terms cover sneaking out of my bed in the dead of night and never calling me again? Because that's the kind of terms we parted on, Harrison."

Harrison nodded as he frowned. "Fair enough. In retrospect, I probably should have told you over breakfast the next day that I knew you weren't the one for me. Would that have been preferable? I tried several times to tell you that night, but you kept refusing to believe me when I said I thought it wasn't working out between us."

Ginny held up a hand. "Let's keep our facts straight, shall we? All men play that resistance game, and you didn't leave me because of me. You left me so you could date Joanna Carver. She was twenty-four and ten years my junior."

"Joanna and I went to dinner once. That was all. It wasn't really dating. She's married now and has forgotten all about me. I wish you had. I was dating other women when we were together. I never hid that fact."

Harrison picked up his water and drank to give himself time to think before he started ranting about jealous women. It worked a little. "Are you admitting you sent the reprimand letter to me and Doris because you're still pissed that you and I broke up?"

"Watch your language in here, mister. If I wanted to, I could have you fined for using profanity in the dining room. I am not your foul-mouthed attorney."

"No, you certainly aren't," Harrison exclaimed. "Because I'm definitely in love with Doris Pearson and I never was in love with you. Is that blunt enough to make you believe me?"

Ginny's loud laughter over his honesty drew everyone's attention. "Let me get this straight. The local Lothario is finally ready to settle down and it just happens to be with the richest single woman in the club. Are you thinking Doris Pearson is going to overlook your sexual transgressions like she did her first husband's? I'm surprised your father didn't latch onto her before you thought of it, but then again, Doris is a lot older than his current wife."

"Okay—time to settle this bill literally and figuratively. I can see now that asking you to meet with me was a bad idea," Harrison said, leaning as far away from her hate as he could.

Both of them were startled when Doris walked up to their table in full attorney regalia, briefcase in hand. His gaze flew to her angry expression at the same time his body caught a whiff of the perfume she evidently only wore to work. Holy hell, he liked it on her. He'd forgotten all about it until now.

"Doris, hi… I…" Harrison hushed immediately when Doris held up a hand. By now that training was firmly in place.

"Since Ms. Wilson doesn't have a house you're interested in buying, I assume you're here trying to woo your way around the club's order for us to stop playing golf together."

"Are you always going to think the worst of me?" Harrison demanded.

Doris narrowed her gaze. "You're having a cozy lunch with a woman everyone knows you've slept with previously. What do you expect me to think, Harrison? You met her behind my back and left it wide open for someone else to call and tell me you were having lunch with her."

"Who called you? And I thought gossip didn't bother you."

Doris lifted her chin. "No one called me, and you're right, it doesn't matter. Nothing I think changes the fact that you can't seem to help feeding the gossip mill every time you turn around. Why didn't you come see me when you got a nastygram from your old flame and see if I got one too?"

Harrison glared back. "I guess for the same reason you didn't tell me about your meeting with your ex-husband… or his new wife."

Ginny's laughter over their fight died instantly when both their angry gazes swung to her.

Doris held out a sheaf of papers. "Here, Ms. Wilson, these are for your reading enjoyment. Since your signature was on the letter I received, I took the liberty of naming you as spokesperson in my lawsuit against the country club. Consider yourself and the Falls Church County Club as having been served with a lawsuit for your actions."

"*Lawsuit?*" Ginny squeaked. "But I didn't do anything illegal."

Doris snorted as she lifted an eyebrow. "Neither did I, but that didn't stop you or the club from threatening me, my sister, and apparently, Harrison. However, it is the club's threatened actions against Lloyd that I found most unconscionable. If you terminate him for accepting green fees from me by credit card, I promise you this club will be paying Lloyd enough in settlement money for him to apply for membership himself when I get done suing on his behalf."

Harrison fought back a sigh. In full mad mode, Doris's effect on his body still defied his understanding. It was a sorry case that she was as mad at him now as she was at Ginny and the club for questioning her innocent actions.

He definitely needed to talk to her more.

He felt sure their communication problems would be non-existent if they were living together.

"Perhaps the club acted in haste. No one thought you would take a little chastisement so seriously," Ginny exclaimed.

Doris smiled and stood as straight as possible so she could stare down at the still seated woman. "You and the other members of this club are attempting to defame my character. As a practicing attorney, I can't leave actions of this sort legally unanswered. Have Lyle give me call at my office to talk about settlement if he's so inclined. If he's not, I'll gladly see you and the other board members in court. My credit card will provide me plenty of receipts for proof, and it will not be difficult to prove every partner I've taken to the course has been a bonafide club member, which is the hard and fast rule. I know the fee schedule is a matter of public record here at the club and frequently gets inspected for juicy tidbits of worthy scandal."

Ginny cleared her throat to speak more clearly. "No one meant to accuse you of…"

When Doris held up a hand, Harrison laughed because Ginny instantly shut up. That was some amazing kind of power Doris exuded, and so far he'd seen it work without exception.

"You're going to want to consult with the club's attorney of record before speaking further to me, Ms. Wilson. I will use anything you say against you if it helps my case. Harrison Graham will be called as a witness to this discussion, and I'm sure I can persuade him to testify against you if needed. You should keep in mind from here on that you're a defendant in a filed court case and act accordingly. This is not a joke."

Harrison grinned as Ginny lifted her ice water with shaking fingers and sipped. He wouldn't be the only witness. Everyone in the dining room had heard what Doris had said to them.

Doris turned to walk away and stopped. She turned back and glared.

"And one more thing… I'm also tired of my mother's

backstabbing games to control my behavior. She does not represent me or my opinions or have any right to pass judgment on my business decisions. As of this moment, I don't care if she supports the club in their actions against me or not. None of you will be my problem for much longer. You may feel free to make it public knowledge to the board that I've contacted Marshall properties about selling my shares to them. I think it's high time this place had some progressive minded management."

Harrison watched until Doris disappeared. "I was a goner the moment that woman spoke to me the first time," he said aloud.

"She's a royal bitch, that's who Doris is," Ginny declared.

Harrison grinned. Doris would have probably considered that a true compliment. "Geez, Ginny… are you planning to write yourself a letter about swearing in the dining room, or are you just planning to discreetly pay the fine? If Doris liked you, she'd give you her freedom of speech lecture. It's quite impressive."

Ginny snorted as she glared at him. "How can you possibly be in love with a woman like her? She hates your guts for simply having lunch with me."

Harrison waved his hand. "No… that's not real jealousy. Doris is still upset about a misunderstanding we had over my realtor. I thought we were past it. Guess we're not. I've obviously got a lot to learn about communicating. Nothing she thinks has ever happened, nor will it, because I belong to her. Maybe I should get a tattoo on my arm that says *Property Of Doris Pearson*. Maybe that will convince her I care."

Harrison stood and put his napkin by the plate he hadn't used. "You need to go to tell Lyle about this as quickly as you can. Doris selling her shares of the club is far more serious than the lawsuit. He'll want to stop her from doing that if he can."

"*Why?* Everyone sells their shares when they leave the club," Ginny demanded.

Harrison shook his head. "Yes, but most sell them *back* to the members of the club. You need to worry in this case because she and her sister Ruth own a whopping fifteen percent each. If Doris leaves, chances are Ruth will leave too. After both their children leave, the Pearsons might be too embarrassed to stay here—which is another five percent traveling away. Of course, I'm going to leave too, and I own yet another five. Just think, Ginny. If we all sold our shares to Marshall Properties, that would give Albert Marshall a whopping forty percent ownership. He would all but own this club single-handedly."

Frowning, Ginny glared harder. "You're trying to dazzle me with your wit because you think you're smarter than the rest of us. What would Doris Pearson gain by selling her stock to a competitor?"

Harrison snorted. "Well, for starters, the current narrow-minded regime would get replaced before any of you could snap the fingers you have stuck up your snooty noses. Doris will surely join the new club and come back here to play golf with whoever the hell she pleases. She's a local pro. Any course would love to say she plays on their greens."

Ginny threw up her hands. "I don't know what's the big deal about this. Not everything in that letter was wrong. Everyone is watching you chase her, Harrison. Primary shareholders are supposed to set the best example of member behavior. Even if you haven't slept with Doris Pearson yet, the ethics committee still has good reasons to be concerned with you two out there on the golf course all the time. People have seen her with her hands all over you."

"Oh, I've slept with Doris, and I intend to do so again, but our intimate relationship has nothing to do with this club, no matter how many people disagree," Harrison declared, grinning like an idiot. He liked saying it out loud. "The truth is that Doris Pearson, who was trained by Babe Zaharias, really has been giving me golf lessons. Anyone playing after us on the course can vouch for that because they've seen her giving me pointers, which includes positioning my body. I'm sure the man the club is threatening to fire will also be more than happy to vouch for that fact in court. Face it, Ginny, the club doesn't stand a snowball's chance in hell against her."

"That's not my fault, and I still shouldn't be named in the lawsuit. This isn't even my vendetta," Ginny complained.

"If you were a complete innocent, you wouldn't have snapped up my lunch invitation so fast. You've had me on the hot seat since we sat down. Look around at all the eyes watching you and all the ears listening to your every mean word. You've caused yourself this public embarrassment. I came to try to help you before it got so complicated."

"I'm not mean, Harrison. How can you say that? Everyone knows I'm not mean," Ginny protested, looking around at diners who were laughing behind their hands. "You have no idea what I've had to live down here being one of Harrison Graham's castoff women."

Harrison leaned to one side and considered Ginny's nervousness. "I know you think I wronged you, but I told you up front I wasn't serious. It's not really my fault you didn't believe my words. Now help me understand why you'd do something like this to me and Doris over some slight that happened between us more than a year ago."

Ginny shook her head. "Haven't you done enough damage to me? If I tell you anything else, I'll have to leave the country club and never show my face here again."

"Maybe. But I think being honest is worth the discomfort. You might at least sleep better at night wherever you are," Harrison said.

Ginny sighed. "I volunteered to send the letter because I thought it would be a good way to get back at you for being so lousy in your treatment of me. But the original idea to chastise Doris wasn't mine... I swear it."

Harrison frowned. "Whose idea was it then?"

"Caroline and Dennis Pearson's... and the Stanton's. The

Stantons don't want Celeste talked about any more than she already is because of her poor taste in husbands. They're campaigning to get Celeste and Avery a new membership here so their daughter isn't socially shut out completely. The problem is that Pearsons are contesting Avery's membership application because of his prior connection to Doris. Plus, the Pearsons don't approve of you, Harrison. You and Doris have turned this club into a scandal shop with your stupid golf games. You two brought this on yourselves."

Harrison snorted at the news. He and Doris had not done a damn thing except play golf and fall in love. "What you're really saying is that screwing with me and Doris was a distraction while the board figures out how to keep peace between two of their richest families."

"No... not... exactly," Ginny hedged, her face flushing with her denial. "You're the one screwing with Doris. You just confessed to it. Everyone else—including her board member parents—simply want her to act like a normal woman her age."

"That's never going to happen, especially if I have any say in the matter," Harrison declared, leaving to go see Lyle himself.

"So did you tell him?" Ruth asked.

Doris shook her head. "Harrison was having lunch with Ginny Wilson without telling me a damn thing about his plans. I decided to return the favor in kind. I told him nothing about mine."

Ruth scooped the hot cookies off the pan and onto a plate. "Doris, you have to tell him."

"No, I don't."

Ruth slid the plate over in front of her smart sister who was not acting smart at the moment. "I can see why Harrison figured it was Ginny behind the letter. I think he was trying to fix it so you wouldn't have to worry about the situation at all."

Doris picked up a cookie and ate half of it in one bite. "Wow, these are great. Explain to me then how Harrison got his current real estate deal to go through in three damn days. He swore he never slept with anyone he did business with, but I'm finding that very hard to believe. He keeps a lot of secrets for an allegedly innocent man."

"You're just mad at Harrison because he was having lunch with Ginny. And you're jealous of his real estate agent, which is so not like you. I guess that means you're really into him."

Doris nodded and pointed at her naïve sister with the rest of her cookie. "Yes, I'm both jealous and mad. But I'm hurt for other reasons too. Ginny Wilson didn't think that letter up alone. She doesn't own enough shares in the company to act without help, and frankly, she's not smart enough to draft something that so carefully skirts the legal line. I could tell this was Mom and Dad, Ruth. If not their idea, you know they were in on it. Next to us, they're the other major shareholders. They would have to approve a letter like that to be mailed out."

Ruth stopped scooping fresh baked cookies off the sheet and nodded. "Yes. It probably was the two of them behind the letter. I for sure know they don't like you playing golf with Harrison. They've been complaining about it since you started. Others think the same thing, but most are old families who don't like anything to change. They complain every time the dining room changes its menu."

Doris nodded as she ate the rest of the cookie in her hand. "You want to know the worst part? I really was giving Harrison golf lessons. He's getting almost good enough to give me a real game. The man has a powerful drive when you can get him to focus on his form. Most of the time he can't concentrate for flirting, but I was making progress with that too."

Doris picked up another cookie and took a bite. Then she finished it off in two bites more before she spoke again. "Wow, these cookies are really good. I may have to have a couple more."

Ruth sighed as she glared. "I think I hate you. You're not even going to get sick, are you?"

Doris stopped chewing. "Am I supposed to get sick?"

"Not necessarily, but most women do," Ruth said, putting two more cookies over on her hungry sister's plate. "It's actually a good thing that you're not. If you're not going to talk to Harrison about this, your good health will keep him from knowing for a while. As tall as you are, you also could hide your baby bump the whole time with some new clothes. If you took a nice, long two month vacation at around seven months, you could keep everyone from knowing."

Doris ate a third cookie and then started on a fourth before feeling guilty. "That would only be delaying the inevitable. When the baby and I came back from wherever we would go for me to deliver in peace, I'd still have to deal with it then. With my luck, this baby will be a boy who looks exactly like Harrison."

"Okay, then. I think you should name your son Leland and list Harrison as the father on the birth certificate. That will at least spread the scandal on both sides of your son's family. If you're going to wear a scarlet letter on your chest over having his child, Harrison Graham should have to wear one too."

"Leland?" Doris asked, pausing mid-bite to consider the name.

Ruth nodded. "Yes. After Dad's brother, our Uncle Leland. He was crazy like you and Harrison. I think it's perfect. Leland Harrison Graham. It sounds very distinguished and important."

Doris put her face in her hand and laughed behind her fingers. Finally, she met her sister's smirking gaze. "God, Ruth. Do you really think Harrison and I are crazy?"

She reached over and snatched another cookie while Ruth was nodding. It would make an even half dozen she'd packed away while she was ranting.

The baby probably was a boy... another Graham messing up her quiet life.

Ruth reached out to smack her sister's sneaking hand with a

spatula. Doris moved fast so she could keep her swiped treat. She laughed at the mock battle with her sister.

"Yes… you are crazy… but it's a good crazy," Ruth declared. "Harrison makes you happy and you make him a better person. Improving his golf game is a prime example."

"You've barely spoken with Harrison. He could be Satan incarnate for all you know. Why do you like him so much?"

Ruth lowered her spatula. "Because Harrison Graham gave my sister the first good sex of her life—and a baby—two things every woman needs to have before she dies. I choose to believe he's reformed. All that time he was sleeping around, he was probably just looking for you anyway. I think you belong together."

Doris sighed. "Where was I when they passed out those female genes of yours? You're as bad as Vivian. I was never that naïve."

"I know," Ruth said unoffended. She *was* happy, had nearly always been happy. "But we're often right. Vivian is sporting a ring now. Freddie popped the question during the last day of finals week. You'll be happy to know she did not let it affect her studies. Instead, it seemed to make her even more determined to graduate with the highest honors possible, even though marriage is all she really wants out of life."

Doris picked up another cookie as she stood to go. "I guess I'm greedy then because I want it all. I like what I do for a living, and I like making my own money. I'm going to need a nanny or two or four to help me. Maybe a housekeeper too. And I'm going to need every penny I can earn if I have to raise my child alone."

Ruth fetched a plastic container and dumped the rest of the cookies into it. There were just a few left of the dozen she'd baked so far. She handed them to her starving pregnant sister who was still stuffing her mouth.

"Here, Doris. You can have it all today, including all the cookies. But also you have to eventually tell Harrison about the baby. It's only fair, and you're the fairest person in our family."

CHAPTER 16

NEARLY A WEEK AND A HALF HAD GONE BY NOW WITHOUT A WORD from the woman he missed like the sun when it wasn't shining.

Doris wasn't taking his calls, and she wouldn't answer her door, which meant she must be really mad about his lunch with Ginny. He'd thought about going to see her at her office, but that would put him in the same desperate category as her slimy ex-husband. He *was* nearly that desperate, but he didn't necessarily want Doris to think so.

He'd been coming by the club every day, even if it was only for a cup of coffee. Putting in an appearance and being social with those gossiping about him and Doris was the best way he'd found to handle the tongue waggers.

He'd even sought out her parents and made them engage in conversation. His bragging glowed with praise about how much better his golf swing had gotten with her tutelage. Beating William McCarthy soundly a couple times had concretely proved his claims. McCarthy had started turning down his invitations, which had dissolved his dicey connection with the kid.

When he saw Doris's golf clubs strapped in the back of a golf cart, his imagination went wicked in a heartbeat. He'd steal her clubs. She'd have to listen to him in order to get them back.

He pulled up and stopped his car directly behind the golf cart. Two seconds later he had her clubs leaning against the trunk of his car ready to be loaded out of sight. Unfortunately remorse hit him in that instant and made him sigh over his planned actions.

Doris loved her damn golf clubs. Could he really stoop this low to get his way with her?

When he heard her voice, he left the bag of clubs and walked back to lean against his front fender to wait for her. Doris appeared shortly with a beaming Vivian by her side. He blatantly eavesdropped with no guilt whatsoever.

"Are you sure you can swing a club with that giant rock on your hand? Watch that you don't get blinded by the sun reflecting off it."

"Stop teasing me, Aunt Doris. You know I never expected anything so big. But isn't Freddie wonderful?"

Vivian's giggle was full of delight and made Harrison smile. Doris's answering laugh had him rubbing his chest. Love was one chest pain after the other for him.

"Yes, Viv. Freddie's a hunky guy with hunky tastes in rings. You're soooooo lucky."

"Why does that sound like sarcasm? Are you teasing me, Aunt Doris?" Vivian demanded, fisting a hand on her hip.

"Yes. I'm teasing. Drive us, will you? My equilibrium is still messed up."

Vivian stuck out her lip. "Mama said you'd been sick. Have you been to the doctor?"

Doris nodded and forced her court smile onto her lips. "Yes… but I'm fine. Nothing to worry about. I'm taking some new vitamins, and Dr. Benson tells me the dizziness will pass soon."

"Good," Vivian declared, then noticed the car parked behind their cart, or rather the handsome man leaning against it. "Hi Harrison! How are you?"

His jig was up. Harrison smiled as he crossed his arms, which wanted nothing more than to be put around the woman trying to pretend she didn't see him.

"Hello, Vivian. I'm fine, thank you. I saw Freddie come in with his father last week. Congratulations on your engagement. Looks like you two are heading to the course. Beautiful day for a golf game," he said, his eyes finally drifting from the girl to the woman beside her.

God, he'd missed Doris. His body tightened on sight and wanted to go to her. Before he could second-guess the instinct, he straightened from the car and walked toward them. He laughed when Doris moved backward and walked around the front of the cart until she was prepped to climb into the passenger seat.

How much longer did she think she could keep avoiding him? They needed to talk things out. "Hi, Doris. Did Lyle get in touch with you?"

"Yes, he did. I'm sure you'll be getting your settlement offer any day now. We were able to reach one that satisfied me. That's why I'm here," Doris said stiffly.

Harrison crossed his arms again and braced his legs as he stared her down. He lifted his chin. "Great. Now that the big hurdle of the club's nosiness is solved, all we need to do is reach a settlement between *us*."

Doris nodded. "Right... I'm actually giving that some thought. I'll call you sometime soon to discuss it."

Harrison narrowed his gaze. "How soon? Are you still avoiding me because I had lunch with Ginny Wilson?"

"Of course not. Perhaps I was slightly mad about you not consulting with me before doing something so ridiculous. However, I soon realized you having lunch with an old flame was actually none of my business. So no... I'm not technically avoiding you, though I can see why you might have thought that. Really, I've just needed some space while I settled some things... uh... legal things."

"Ginny Wilson is an old friend, not an old flame," Harrison denied.

Doris snorted and shook her head. "From what I heard, I would say the evidence points to a different conclusion. A man doesn't usually sneak away from the bed of *an old friend*."

Harrison rubbed his nose and sighed. He glanced and saw Vivian's face turning pink. He glared at Doris for involving her bright and shiny niece in their too adult discussion.

"I see. Did you hear the entire conversation between me and Ginny?"

"Nearly all of it," Doris said carefully, not wanting him to know how she'd paused in shock when she'd seen them sitting at the table together. "But then I imagine most of the dining room did as well. You two were yelling at each other pretty loudly. It was impossible not to hear."

Harrison dropped his head and groaned. He seemed destined to mess up with this woman. "That's not going to stop you from calling me soon though, right?"

"No. It absolutely will not stop me," Doris vowed, her gaze seeking out Vivian's and not holding Harrison's. "Ready to go, Viv? If we don't hurry, we'll have to let the next set of golfers play through."

Vivian bit her lip as she finger-waved at Harrison. "Okay. Bye, Harrison," she said.

"Bye, Vivian. Nice to see you again," Harrison replied.

He sighed as he watched them drive off. His mind churned on how strange Doris was acting around him. She didn't seem really mad in the normal sense, but then she wasn't a normal woman. If he didn't stay on his toes, she managed to talk her way around him.

No. Her mood was far worse than mad. Doris seemed to be looking for any good reason she could find to avoid interacting with him. That was what he did when he wanted to extricate himself from a relationship that had run its course.

He was still standing there trying to puzzle it out when a caddy he knew pulled up in another cart and took the slot Doris and Vivian had just zoomed out of. After saying hello, Harrison sadly walked back to his car and reluctantly slid into the driver's seat to move the vehicle out of the cart loading zone.

His mind was still on his conversation with Doris when he put the car into gear and backed up. A giant thump and a few crunches later, he swore, closed his eyes, and laid his head down on the steering wheel.

Their confrontation had distracted him so much he'd forgotten all about his original plan to steal her golf clubs and hold them hostage. Now he'd likely killed them... if the crunch was any indication. He may have also killed his last hope of convincing Doris he wasn't as bad as she thought he was.

He saw Vivian driving straight toward him. Their golf cart slid to a stop beside his car. He'd wanted to force Doris to talk to him, but this sure wasn't what he'd had in mind.

With a sigh of resignation, Harrison climbed out of his car.

Doris groaned as she stooped and picked out what was left of a favorite driver from the mangled pile of clubs. The bag had a large black tire mark on it and the shoulder strap was torn. It could probably be repaired, but the ends of all the clubs had been destroyed when Harrison backed over them.

She glared up at him as he stood over her contemplating the damage. His well-developed arm muscles strained inside his rolled up sleeves. Just looking at him made her want sex. It wasn't fair. Why couldn't he have been the one she'd married all those years ago? She'd have had twenty years of good sex by her age.

Instead, Harrison had been a child when she'd married Avery. Now years later, the good-looking, golf-club-killing bastard had accidentally fathered her child.

And he'd killed her golf clubs in yet another accident. Even without trying, Harrison Graham had a real talent for messing up her life in every way he possibly could.

"I'm very sorry, Doris. I'll replace your clubs with the best ones money can buy," Harrison promised, expecting her to break out in tears when the shock of what he'd done wore off.

Doris rose to face down the man who'd murdered her favorite reminder of the only past she was proud of. "You can never replace these clubs, Harrison. They were a gift to me from George Zaharias. His wife Babe was five foot seven. Like nearly all women golfers, I was playing with clubs sized for someone like her. George made me use his one day and I discovered men's clubs fit me much better. George insisted I keep the set he'd given me to use. Babe gave me the red bag for them because George had hated the color. He said he thought bright red was too girlie."

So Babe Zaharias and her husband had given Doris the clubs. Harrison hung his head and studied the ground. *Damn.* It was worse than he thought.

"Harrison, there's something about the demise of my golf clubs I don't understand," Doris said sharply as she studied the repentant man standing in front of her.

Trained to focus, Doris noted, but ignored the crowd gathering around the two of them. She heard Vivian whispering an explanation over and over as more and more people came to observe. Soon the entire club would be out here in the parking lot listening to her and Harrison argue. They were providing yet more scandalous grist for the club's gossip mill.

Doris lifted her chin. "How did my clubs get behind your car? I know I strapped them into our golf cart. Vivian and I loaded our clubs at the same time."

Harrison nodded as he raised his head. Regrets would render him mute if he didn't confess immediately. He sighed to see Vivian's concerned gaze bouncing back and forth between them.

"Okay, you caught me. I moved your clubs. I was going to hold them hostage until you talked to me."

"This is unbelievable," Doris said, shaking her head slowly side-to-side.

Harrison huffed out an exasperated breath. "Why? I got desperate. You've been avoiding me, and I've missed you every damn day. I swear on my life I never meant to hurt your golf clubs. Backing over them truly was an accident. I was distracted by our earlier conversation and forgot to right my original sin. I climbed into my car and forgot they were even back there."

Doris lifted both hands skyward. Her voice rose as she spoke. "That's not the definition of an accident, Harrison. That's called stealing and getting caught red-handed. Haven't you changed my life enough already?"

Harrison drew in a breath and rocked on his heels. "No, I haven't. If you want to know the whole truth, I was hoping I could eventually talk you into marrying me. However, I was planning to tell you so with less of an audience to witness my craziness."

"*Marry you?* That's a pretty drastic measure to take just to make me forget about you destroying my one-of-a-kind golf clubs."

Harrison snorted. "It would be considered drastic except for the fact I've been thinking about marrying you since the night of the dance. And like I said... running over your clubs was an accident. The stealing part... okay, I guess you have a point and I need to make that right too. What can I do to pay for my misdeeds, *Judge Pearson?*"

Doris rubbed a hand over her face. "Drop the sarcasm and give me your golf clubs."

"*My golf clubs?*" Harrison repeated in surprise.

"Did I stutter? Yes. I want your damn golf clubs. Get them for me right now. I'll take your clubs as restitution for mine. If you manage to find a replacement set that suits me, then I'll return yours to you. In the meantime, at least I can play golf today. The green fees are already paid."

"Fine." Harrison fetched his keys from the ignition and unlocked the trunk. He drew out his clubs and handed them over. Doris shouldered the bag like it weighed nothing and proudly carried them to her rented golf cart. She fastened his pristine black and white bag in the back. It was a stark contrast to Vivian's pink canvas one.

"Okay, Viv. Problem solved. Let's go," Doris said, climbing into the passenger side, eyes forward as she waited. She was not going to look at him again. They'd already given their audience more than enough to chew on.

The club would be buzzing with this story forever. Harrison may have just replaced his father as Falls Church most notorious Graham.

When Vivian turned to him with big eyes, Harrison nodded and motioned her to the cart with his hand. The girl nodded and scrambled into the driver's seat.

His frown followed them all the way to the first hole. By the time the cart parked out on the green, all their eavesdroppers had dispersed to take the story inside the club where it could really travel with some speed.

Lost in mourning his mistake, Harrison wasn't expecting the firm slap on his shoulder that snapped his attention back to the present and had his head turning.

"Look on the bright side, Mr. Graham. At least Ms. Pearson doesn't hate you for everything," Lloyd declared.

"She doesn't? How can you tell that, Lloyd?" Harrison asked.

Lloyd chuckled before replying. "Ms. Pearson took your golf clubs instead of asking for an obscene amount of money. She could have made sure you publicly suffered if she'd wanted. Though, come to think of it, you kind of did that to yourself by announcing your intentions to marry her. But hey... cheer up, Mr. Graham. She's out there on the course playing with your driver, right at this very moment. It's sort of like you two are going steady now."

Harrison reluctantly laughed. "That's a fine thought, Lloyd. I wish I could be that optimistic, but I killed her beloved golf clubs. You heard her story. I took her past away with their death. She has to hate me now."

Lloyd stooped to the mangled bag and lifted it. He slid the bent clubs back inside the leather. "You know, I could tell you were sweet on her the first day you two went out to play. Ms. Pearson's a fine woman—probably the finest that ever walked through the doors of this place."

Harrison sighed loudly. "Yes, I know. Recently, I've realized that I've done some pretty mean things to women, but I don't think I've ever messed up this badly before."

"Mean things? You mean like sneaking out on Ms. Wilson?"

"Did the gossip committee post that one on the bulletin board?" Harrison asked.

Lloyd laughed at the teasing. "No, sir. I was taking my lunch break in the back of the dining room. I heard that one for myself, even all the way back there. Ms. Pearson was right about all the witnesses."

"Figures. The woman is damned near always right. My life was real simple before I got it in my head that I had to have Doris Pearson be part of it."

Lloyd shook his head and grinned. "Love makes a man crazy and you aren't the first one to travel that road. I've been down it a few times myself. But concerning your real problem, I can help you replace her golf clubs. These clubs were pretty standard ones twenty years ago. Worse case, the replacement set will be a special order and maybe slightly used, but I'm pretty sure I can get you a nearly identical set within a few weeks."

"Seriously?" Harrison asked, feeling some real hope.

"Seriously," Lloyd said firmly. "I could probably find another bag too, but if I were you, I'd fix this one since it's special to her.

That spine can be fixed if you're handy with a leather punch. Some leather cleaner ought to be able to remove the road dirt and bring it back to life the rest of the way."

"I'm going to owe you for life, Lloyd," Harrison said with sincerity.

"No, you won't. Your future wife saved my job and fought for my integrity. She's the most righteous person I've ever met. There isn't much I wouldn't do for Ms. Pearson."

"Great. Will you tell her she should marry me then? Falling in love with her has ruined my reputation."

Lloyd laughed as he stowed the red bag and broken clubs in the still open trunk of the car. "First chance I get, Mr. Graham. First chance I get, I will put in a good word for you."

CHAPTER 17

THE KITCHEN WAS THE FIRST ROOM HE'D FINISHED. NOW THE master bedroom was done and it was the place he stored most of his stuff. The closets were packed with boxes, but he'd get it all put away eventually.

There were nine more rooms to renovate. He was going to be here for at least a year if he didn't hire help.

Stripped down to his sleeveless undershirt, Harrison was hand-sanding the drywall repairs he'd made in the living room. He told himself he was saving all kinds of money doing the work alone, but the real truth was that the manual labor made him at least tired enough to sleep at night. Otherwise, he stared at the ceiling, obsessing about the woman who was still mad at him.

The semi-broken doorbell sounded weakly throughout the house. He might not have heard it over the gravelly sound of his sanding if he hadn't been standing in the living room so near his front door. Since no one knew he'd moved in but his father, his thought was that Angela had finally driven his still recovering dad by to see it.

Harrison pulled open the door to find Doris standing on his stoop. "Hello," he said, taking in her formal outfit. He wondered how much of his relief showed on his face. "Nice suit, Ms. Pearson. Nicer legs."

Doris swallowed and glanced down at her clothes before raising her gaze back to his. She'd come straight from work. "Thank you. It was court day. I had to dress like this."

Her gaze glued itself to sleek, muscled arms and wide shoulders that tapered down to a waist made for a woman's hands to grip—her hands knew that intimately. Most of him was covered in white dust, and yet she still wanted to jump into his arms.

Doris cleared her throat, hoping to clear away the lust she was feeling. But wasn't that why she was here? She raised her eyes to his and made them stay there.

"I talked to your…" She stumbled over choosing the proper address since the woman was younger than even the man standing in front of her. "I talked your stepmother into telling me where your new house was. I cornered her and your father at the club yesterday. Your father was perfectly charming, but he kept laughing every time I tried to ask any kind of question about you. I hate to admit it, but going into lawyer mode didn't faze him. Frankly, I hope I never have to examine him during a trial."

Harrison laughed at her teasing. "Angela must have felt sorry for you having to deal with Dad. Dad was probably giving you a hard time because I found you first. He thinks you're a good catch. I let him get by with saying that nonsense because he was having a heart attack when we discussed you. When he gets well, I may have to kick his ass."

Doris shook her head. "Perhaps in his world view of women I am a catch. Not many men would agree with him. Your father isn't like you much, though—or rather you're not much like him," she said, then promptly stopped discussing that train of thought before it derailed her visit completely.

Her sigh was long and loud. "May I come in, Harrison? The neighbors were already nervous when I pulled into your driveway and got out of my car wearing a suit. Now I feel them staring at my back."

"Sure. Of course," Harrison said quickly, stepping aside so Doris could walk by his dirty body and stay clean. Her perfume hit his nose and his lonely dick reacted instantly. She had on the secret scent she only wore to work. Damn, he liked it. "Be careful in here. It's very dusty. I've been sanding drywall."

Doris nodded and glanced into the cavernous white room to the right of the foyer. "This house is very nice. I can see why you set your sights on buying it. It's very appealing."

Harrison looked into the room and shrugged. All he saw at the moment was the long list of work still to be done. "This is not a home yet, but I'm sure it will be for someone one day. That's my goal. I buy cheap, do the repairs, and then sell the house for a profit. It's hard work, but it pays off financially and mentally."

"And now I know what you do for a living," Doris said, smiling.

Harrison laughed and shook his head. "Actually, I don't usually do my own manual labor. I hire it done. In addition to renovating and reselling houses, I also own about a hundred vending machines spread across town, two full service Laundromats, and a movie theater. This is my third house investment. Come on... I'll give you a tour. I've finished two rooms already."

Doris reached out and grabbed his firm arm before he could walk away from her. Muscles bunched and tightened beneath her grip. Her mind forgot everything except that magical thing leaping between them as it always did.

She finally heard one of them moaning. When his mouth closed over hers and cut off the sound she was making, she realized the origin had been her own throat. Her arms didn't know anything else except how good he felt when they closed around him in relief. She moaned in complaint when Harrison pulled his lips away from hers.

"I've missed you like crazy, but I'm getting you filthy. You'll be ruined if we don't stop this right now," he whispered.

Snickering because she knew it was far too late to worry about him ruining her, Doris closed her eyes and gripped the waistband of his jeans as his fingers slipped bobby pins from her French twist. Once released her hair fell to her shoulders and then both his hands plowed through it. He kissed her face and laughed in each ear as garbled sounds of gratitude continually escaped her throat.

She didn't care about dust on her suit any more than she'd cared about the grass stains on her dress. She didn't care about anything except that Harrison Graham didn't stop kissing her.

"Harrison… I've missed you too," she whispered back, admitting her feelings to them both.

His lips brushed over hers hard and hot. She met them eagerly to return his enthusiasm.

Harrison's lips drifted away for good as his hand slipped down to lace her fingers through his. He used their connection to tug her along. "We'll look at the kitchen later. All I can think about right now is showing you the master bedroom. I need a detour into the shower though before I ruin you further."

"Can I at least watch while I wait? I promise that won't ruin anything."

Doris actually blushed when Harrison stopped walking and his hot gaze met hers again.

"Woman—I want to marry you. I have from the first time we talked. Before this goes any further, I need to know if you're going to take my proposal seriously. I don't want more unforgettable sex to have to get over if you decide to kick me to the curb when you're done with me."

Doris dropped her gaze from his to study the floor. "I think my double decade lousy marriage proves I'm not the kind of woman to kick a man to the curb unless I have a damn good reason. But I do have my reservations about us. What if the life we have together doesn't work out the way you think it will, Harrison? Sex gets old… even great sex… or so I hear from my divorce clients."

"That won't matter in our relationship because this isn't about the sex. Hell, I'm a dumb guy, but even I know what we have is more," Harrison exclaimed. "This is about wanting you in my life and missing you when you're not with me. The sex is just… okay the sex is damn amazing, I won't lie. But we've got a lot more going on here. Can't you tell?"

"Yes, but… I guess I'm afraid," Doris whispered.

"Of me?" Harrison whispered back in alarm, appalled at the idea.

"No," Doris declared firmly, snorting over the denial. "I'm scared of losing you. I'm scared of not being the woman you need. I've never been good at being a girl, Harrison. I made you give me your golf clubs *and* I used them to play a damn good game even though I was pissed at you the whole time. I also meant what I said about not giving them back. I'm as hard ass as any man you've ever met."

Harrison frowned because he knew it was what Doris expected. As if he'd jeopardize their relationship over a set of stupid golf clubs. Hell, he'd buy her a factory that made them if it was what it took to keep her.

"Okay. If I can't convince you that your girlie side is safe with me, then we'll be men together. We'll wear matching golf polos at the club, and I'll let it be known that it's kinky foreplay leading up to the best sex of my life. I'll say you like to wear my tidy-whiteys under those knee length pencil skirts that show off your sexy legs. Let people think what they will, honey. I just want you to be mine."

Doris choked out a laugh. "You really would tell people that crap, wouldn't you? You'd be embarrassed, but you'd do it for the shock and awe."

"Doll, there isn't much I wouldn't do for you… or to you. I'm open-minded. Just don't ask me to share you with another man. I want you all to myself. I'm greedy as hell when it comes to being the man in your bed."

Her fingers found their way to his chest to grip his shirt. She pulled his mouth to hers, kissed him hard, and let go. "Shut up. You know I'm jealous of your damn realtor. And if I see you at lunch again with any woman you've slept with previously, I swear I will make both your lives a living hell."

Harrison stared down at her mouth, which was still wet with his kisses. His already tight jeans instantly became torturous. "I believe you. It was a living hell when you stopped talking to me. That was all the punishment I could stand. But I won't say we'll never fight over anything. For example, I still want to know what the doctor said about your dizzy spells. I've just found you, Doris. I can't lose you now. If you're sick, I want you to tell me. I have money too. We'll find someone to make you better."

Shock at his demand to help her had her pushing away. In her lust, she'd forgotten what she'd come to tell him. Before she could open her mouth, though, the doorbell rang. Or at least she thought it was the doorbell. "What is that? It sounds like a wounded goose."

Harrison snickered. "It's the damn doorbell. I haven't had time to look at it yet." He stared at her high color. "Your jacket is covered in drywall dust now."

Doris unbuttoned the jacket and slipped it off. She folded it primly over her arm. Her silky white blouse didn't do a good job of hiding the new white lace bra she had on under it. Harrison's interested gaze heated her from her head to her toes. Okay. Shower. Sex. Then she'd tell him about the baby.

The wounded goose honked again and made her giggle at how bad it sounded. "Get the door and put that poor animal out of its misery."

Harrison sighed. "Are you sure? I have no idea who it is. I thought you were Dad and you weren't."

"Yes. Answer it. It won't change my intentions," Doris vowed.

"That's not been my luck lately," Harrison warned.

"I promise this time," Doris said, crossing one finger in an X over her chest. His gaze followed her finger around her breasts and made her smile.

Harrison trudged back the ten feet they'd managed down his hallway and pulled open the door. The woman immediately came inside and waved a thick manila envelope in her hand.

"Hi, Harrison. I was showing another home in the neighborhood. Here are your copies of the paperwork on the house, including all inspections. Oh…"

Doris tilted her head as the older woman's gaze landed squarely on her.

Harrison sighed. "Marigold, this is the Honorable Doris Pearson, my…" He paused and looked at the woman he loved waiting for her to supply the term she preferred.

"His girlfriend… I'm his girlfriend," Doris finished. She returned Harrison's pleased smile. "I don't care if it is 1965, buddy. If you ever introduce me as your 'old lady', we're done."

Harrison chuckled over her threat. His joke about kinky foreplay hadn't been too off the mark. Their verbal skirmishes revved him up every time. "Doris, this is Marigold Hamilton. She's the realtor who sold me this house."

Doris looked at the gray-haired woman. She was old enough to be Harrison's mother… or maybe even hers. This was the woman who'd inspired her jealous rant about him sleeping his way to a deep discount. Her mouth twitched seeing the humor in her stupidity, but she didn't dare start laughing. She wouldn't stop and Harrison would torture her over it forever.

"It's very nice to meet you, Ms. Hamilton. This is an amazing house."

Marigold nodded. "Yes. It's wonderful, and I'm so happy Harrison's bid was accepted." Her gaze went to Harrison, who was still mostly covered in dust. "Oh my… I see I've interrupted your renovating work. Well, I'll be going now. Call me if you find anything missing from your copies of the paperwork."

With a wave of her hand, Marigold disappeared back out the door.

"When were you going to tell me the woman's age?" Doris demanded.

Harrison threw the deadbolt before he turned around. He tried unsuccessfully not to grin. "Probably never," he admitted.

"Well, here's what I think about that fact." Doris lifted her middle finger, glared at Harrison, and then stalked off down the massively long hallway.

"Invitation accepted, Ms. Pearson. I plan to do exactly that as soon as I get clean," Harrison promised, laughing as he quickly covered the distance between him and the woman he wanted.

WHEN WATCHING HADN'T BEEN ENOUGH to keep her patient, she'd stripped and joined Harrison in the shower. Now the front of her was pressed against cool tile while Harrison pressed hot, hungry kisses across her shoulders. Her whimpering echoed off the walls as he joined their bodies and pulled her face around to his to kiss her, his tongue in her mouth mimicking what was happening elsewhere.

There was a bone-deep satisfaction in letting Harrison do whatever he wanted to her. Plus, she trusted him to lead her down a path that would satisfy both of them. God knew, he hadn't steered them wrong yet.

Pleasure weakened her legs when a climax hit several minutes later, but Harrison was right there to keep her standing while he took the rest of what he wanted as well. He was breathing heavily in her ear when he was done, but his mouth pressed hotly to her neck as if they hadn't even started yet. He made her feel womanly and needed and sexy. He made her wish this really could be her everyday life.

"I love you," Harrison rasped, his voice rough with barely sated desire.

Doris heard herself make a squeak of alarm when his hands cupped her breasts tightly. She felt owned by the man still throbbing in her depths. Maybe she was.

"I love you too," she whispered back, groaning when one hand left her breasts and slid down the front of her.

Suddenly, she was away from the wall and turned until the warm water of the shower sluiced down her front. Her hands dangled lifelessly over the muscular arms holding her in the water's path. The roving hand slipped between her legs to massage as he slipped out of her from behind.

No wonder he'd gotten her pregnant. All she could think about with Harrison was doing this again and again.

His teeth nipped at her neck while his hand cupped her. She made no move to get away or to stop him. There wasn't much she wouldn't let him do to her body. Worse, she had no desire to escape. If she stayed with him, there'd no doubt be more children than just the one she carried. If she stayed, the man would torment her until she couldn't think straight. It was strange how happy that thought made her.

"Mine," he said firmly.

As his large hand covered everything between her legs, Doris nodded at his statement, still mute. His sexy growl of approval in her ear had her quivering in his arms. After another minute or two went by, then she felt him remove his hand to turn the water off.

Doris sighed and turned around to face her talented lover at last. She lifted a hand to Harrison's now clean face. Water ran off his chiseled jaw and down her fingers. "I don't know what to do about you. Would you consider living in sin with me?"

Harrison's snort under her fingertips answered before he did.

"No. I want to be your husband. I want to put a ring on your hand. My grandfather would come back from his grave and kick my ass if I did anything other than that."

Doris sighed as she shook her head. "I can't think about marriage yet. I just got divorced. Divorcing was awful."

"Draw up a marriage contract then. Put in whatever terms you need to feel safe. I'll sign it," Harrison said as he stepped out of his shower and dripped across the floor to fetch towels.

"You're soaking the floor. Did it ever occur to you to gather up towels before you got in here?" she asked.

"Nagging already? Are you planning to domesticate me?" Harrison asked. He mock-glared as he put one towel on the floor for her to stand on it. "Get out here, woman."

Doris felt one eyebrow rise. "Really? And if I don't jump at the command?"

Snickering at her resistance, Harrison held out a hand to her. "I'm sorry. You're right. I'm being rude... especially after what we just did. *Please* get the hell out here, " he amended.

Giggling at his fake apology, Doris stepped out and let Harrison wrap an enormous fluffy towel around her. He kissed her hard and hotly as he gathered her and the towel into his arms. She could tell he was contemplating round two. She was contemplating whether or not she could keep him interested long-term.

"The legal document is called a pre-nuptial agreement," she said softly.

Harrison shrugged. "In my mind, it's called the doing-whatever-the-hell-it-takes-to-marry-Doris document. We can live in your house, or I'll buy you a house. All I care is that we're together wherever we are," he said, hugging her still compliant body against his.

It was quiet in the bathroom, and she barely heard the wounded goose honking again. When it rang a second time and sounded even worse, her face creased with a grin. Harrison's large body sighed heavily around hers as he heard it too. His reaction made her giggle harder. She was giddy again.

"That has to be Dad and Angela this time," he said. "They're the only ones who'd be that persistent."

Doris tucked her head against his wet shoulder and laughed, highly amused about his irritated tone. He wanted to be alone with her. The smile on her face as she absorbed the fact felt permanent. Dealing with interruptions and work around Harrison just felt so normal. She found herself wondering if her sister always felt this way about her husband and family. She really hoped she did.

His sigh echoed in the bathroom. "I have to answer it. He'll just keep ringing until I do… and you can bet he's seen your car in the driveway and knows you're here."

Doris nodded. "It's okay, Harrison. Let me get the dust off my skirt and then I'll be right out."

Harrison nodded. "Are you always such a good sport?"

Doris shrugged. "Probably not—but I am after great sex."

Harrison grinned at her admission. "You're a rare female, Ms. Pearson. Make sure you put a requirement for great sex in our pre-nuptial agreement. Truly, I want to give you that for the rest of our lives. The idea of being with you every day thrills me more than any business deal I've ever made."

Doris sighed heavily as a naked and still wet Harrison exited the master bathroom. What in the world had she done to capture the handsome man's interest like she had? His backside flexing as he walked drew another sigh from her. Now, she really was wanting another round. How long would life with him be this way?

Harrison was going to age well and only get sexier. Worrying now about Angela seeing him the way she did, she could only hope Harrison had stopped in the bedroom for proper clothes before answering the door. In the irritated mood he was in, the man was unpredictable. It wasn't hard to imagine Harrison not bothering to dress himself.

The dust came off her summer weight wool skirt much easier than she'd imagined, which gave her mind plenty of time to dwell on her cowardice. She promised herself that she'd find the right opening after his father and Angela left to tell Harrison about the baby.

Harrison's willingness to sign a pre-nuptial agreement had finally been evidence enough to convince her that the man wanted her in a way no other man in her life ever had. Maybe if she gave it enough thought, she'd eventually wrap her head around the idea of being his wife.

CHAPTER 18

"Did you tell him yet?" Ruth asked, setting the short glass on the table and adding a votive candle.

"No. His father and stepmother came right after we got out of the shower. I had things to do so I left before they did," Doris said.

A giggling Ruth leaned closer and asked in a whisper. "Tell me more about the shower. Skip the father stuff."

Doris giggled. "Did you invite me here to question me about my vastly improved sex life?"

Ruth picked up a bag of shiny circle confetti. "No, of course not—that's merely a perk. Since you were coming to talk to Lyle again, who's just down the hall, I wanted to check and see if you were still getting dizzy. If you hadn't forgiven Harrison for killing your golf clubs, which it seems like you have, I was going to talk you into it."

Doris smiled. "Forgive is not quite the right word, but Harrison made restitution without complaining. It would be churlish of me to hold a grudge. Honestly, I rather like playing with his clubs."

"Of course, you do," Ruth teased, as she shoved a bag of confetti into her grinning sister's hand. "Stop thinking about your sexy boyfriend's equipment and sprinkle these on the tables. Pretend it's magical fairy dust. Use it sparingly. I have to decorate twenty more."

Doris stared at her sister. "Ruth—you know I'm a realist. I'm not qualified to sprinkle fairy dust." She sighed at her sister's twinkling gaze. "Yes, I still get dizzy, but it's not bad so long as I eat more often. I'm carrying snacks in my briefcase now, trying to ward off the blood sugar dips. I'm going to be as big as a house by the time I deliver. I hope you're happy."

Ruth giggled. "Of course, I'm happy. I'm just surprised you're in such a good mood about it. Harrison killed your beloved golf clubs and yet he still lives and well—exhibit A—you shared the shower. I know from my own experience that kind of sex is pretty magical. So throw some confetti, Ms. Realist. Spread that shower joy around."

Doris snorted and looked at the shiny circles again. She thought of Harrison's confiscated golf clubs and how they were balanced way better than her old ones. "I discovered his 8 iron is top of the line. It performs better than anything I've ever used to play a hole."

"It must be top of the line, given what he managed to accomplish with it," Ruth declared firmly.

Doris felt heat climb her face as her sister's laughter echoed in the empty banquet room. Blushing over innuendo? Good Lord, what was next? "Oh, stop it, Ms. Dirty Mind. I was talking about Harrison's damn lofting iron."

When Ruth's laughter got even louder, Doris rolled her eyes and shut up.

"Teasing you is so much fun. Tim said to thank you for inspiring me lately. We've been like teenagers again. I think I'm just happy you're happy at last. I hope this never changes for either of us."

Doris sighed and threw a handful of shiny gold circles across the table. They mostly landed in a clump. She also had to pick several circles out of the votive candle vase where airborne ones had decided to land. The last thing she needed was to be the cause of a fire at the country club. She was already in deep doo-doo for stirring up a legal fuss.

Ruth's chuckle had her glaring, but her sister slipped the confetti bag from her fingers. "This ought to be good. You're no more domesticated than Harrison is. Living together will be an adventure for both of you."

Doris shrugged, unable to deny it. "Harrison doesn't want us to live together. He wants us to get married."

Ruth stopped, stared, and then blinked. "Married? He already proposed? Wow... that was fast. What's it been? Barely two months, right?"

Doris sighed. "I refuse to think of how short a time I've known him. In his mangled way—yes, Harrison has proposed. Best of all, he did so without knowing what's happened. He's even willing to let me draw up a pre-nuptial agreement so I can protect my finances. I'm running out of arguments, Ruth."

"So are you going to do it then? Are you going to marry the infamous womanizer, Harrison Graham, and take him off the market?"

Doris shrugged and dipped her chin to her chest. "I'm contemplating what that would be like. I've only been divorced a few months. How can I marry again so soon? It gives me the willies even thinking about it. Not many things do that to me."

Ruth narrowed her gaze and pointed at her older sister's still flat stomach. "Think of Leland and get over it. That should be reason enough to ignore other decorum in this situation."

"I suppose," Doris groaned. "*Leland.* You and your boy names. It could be a girl, you know."

Ruth threw confetti and laughed. "Okay. Call her Harriet Rose after her father."

Doris groaned louder and then laughed. "No. I could never do that to a child. I'd probably call her Rue... after you."

Ruth put a hand on her chest and sniffled. "Rue... that's so sweet. I love that name."

They chatted away for the two hours it took Ruth to decorate the rest of the tables. Doris ended up sitting at most of them. Near the end, she ended up rummaging in her briefcase for a bag of peanuts to munch on.

They were nearly done when they heard a woman yelling in the hall. Then Doris heard a voice she recognized all too well.

SHE AND RUTH walked out of the room and followed the arguing to just outside Lyle's office. Avery and Celeste were faced off and still yelling.

"This is all your fault. I had everything worked out. They were going to let us join until you lost your temper," Celeste declared.

"I don't see why I have to start all over as if I've never been a member here before. I don't have time to be gathering reference letters and jumping through social hoops. I thought you said your parents had as much clout here as the Pearsons."

"They do," Celeste declared. "But nobody likes you, Avery. You're not always nice to people and things like this are the consequences."

"Oh, like you're a saint?" Avery said, glaring at his wife. "Bet good old Mom and Dad would love knowing their daughter was a slut who'd slept with two men at once."

Celeste drew in a breath and raised a hand to her mouth. "I did that for you. It was your idea. And you have no right to call me such names."

Avery snorted and shook his head. "My idea was to get you pregnant so your parents would accept our marriage. I couldn't do that on my own by being nice. I figured you'd be making plans to foist the baby off on a nanny so we could have a normal life after it comes."

"You really don't want this baby at all, do you?" Celeste demanded, tears leaking now from both eyes.

"No. I never did," Avery admitted. "I think you're fine enough as a wife… when you're not being whiny. Why are you crying? It wasn't like you were a virgin when I met you, Celeste. You've gotten around as much as I have and I'm nearly twice your age. You know how life really is."

Celeste put a hand over her stomach. "Legally, this child is yours, Avery."

"But biologically it's not mine. All I need is a paternity test to prove my lack of involvement. No court in the world would make me pay for a child that wasn't mine."

"You don't know for certain it's not yours," Celeste challenged.

"Yes I do. I got the mumps at sixteen and never knocked up any female I slept with. That makes me pretty damn certain, little girl. I may be a bastard, but I'm not going to be raising any of my own," Avery exclaimed.

Shocked at his callousness to his young wife, Doris walked forward to step between them. She'd heard what he'd said, but part of her mind couldn't yet believe it. All this time… she'd thought the problem was her.

Avery and Celeste both winced as she stepped between them. She turned and put a hand on Celeste's shoulder, forcing the young woman to make eye contact. "Are you okay?"

Celeste shook her head. "No, Ms. Pearson. I'm not okay, but what choice do I have except to deal with him? I brought this all on myself—just like Avery said."

Doris tightened her grip for a moment. "Avery is being an insensitive ass, but that's doesn't change the truth of your story. You need to hang tough for the sake of your child. You have more recourse than I can share standing here in the hallway."

She let go and reached into her briefcase. Fishing around, she finally pulled out a card stuck in one of its many pockets.

She held it out to Celeste. "Here. This is my friend, Marcus

Gooding. Give him a call. Tell him Doris referred you. He excels at all kinds of family law. I'll call him and pave the way so he can start putting together a case for you."

When Celeste swiped at her tear-filled eyes and nodded, Doris reached into her briefcase for a couple tissues and handed them over. She kept them for clients. Most betrayed women wept with the hurt.

"Thank you, Ms. Pearson. You're a real class act. No one will ever convince me otherwise," Celeste said, dabbing at her eyes.

A vicious snort had Doris turning to face down the man who'd repeatedly betrayed her.

"Getting even with me, Doris? I thought you didn't believe in revenge. Graham finally drag you down from that ivory tower you locked yourself away in all these years?"

Doris glared at the man she'd married. She thought Avery had been bad before the divorce. He was deplorable now. "Avery, I think you've said enough. You should leave before things get really ugly."

Avery snorted. "That's it? That's all you got? Hell, anyone can throw around a few ultimatums. You used to be a fireball with that tongue of yours. Graham tame that too?"

Doris looked at the weeping woman by her side. "May I?"

"Sure," Celeste declared, shooting a look of hatred at her husband. "If murder wasn't illegal, I'd kill him myself. But apparently I'm the only person willing to take care of my baby."

Ignoring the crowd gathering at both ends of the hallway, Doris looked over at her sister. Ruth strode forward with purpose. She took the briefcase Doris passed to her and put a protective arm around Celeste, leading the woman away.

Doris waited until Celeste was safely tucked among friends before she turned back to the man she had regretted knowing for most of her life. "You lied to John Benson. You knew all along that you couldn't have children. You could have told all of us that at any time. I had test after test after test and you never said a word about what you knew. I even had exploratory surgery, Avery. They cut me open to check things out. And all that time… there was nothing wrong with me at all, was there?"

"How should I know? I'm not a doctor. Ask John like you always do."

Doris glared. Hate for the man in front of her grew. He wasn't even sorry. To Avery, their relationship had just been a game he played for the money prizes she dropped on him out of guilt. "Why would you do that, Avery?"

"Think about it, Doris. Would you have stayed with me if you knew I was sterile?" Avery demanded.

Doris nodded. "Yes. Just like I stayed when you were cruel, perverted, and repeatedly unfaithful. Sterility would have only made me feel more loyal to you. Now, all I can think is that for twenty years I could have gotten pregnant if I'd taken the kind of chances you took."

"But you didn't… and I knew you wouldn't," Avery said, lifting a hand. "Immaculate conception is a hard one to pull off, even for the high and mighty Doris Pearson. You have to have sex to get pregnant, sweetheart."

"Actually," Doris said, leaning toward him until she was inches from his face. "All it took was a virile man who truly knew how to please a woman in bed. Harrison was so terrific, I couldn't get enough of him. Now here I am, caught by surprise, carrying his child at age 43. I thought it was a miracle. Today I found out differently, though, didn't I?"

"You're pregnant? Good God. Bet Graham's mortified to know how he slipped up with you of all people. You're an old lady, Doris. Why don't you take one of your little trips to Europe and solve this problem?"

Doris clinched her fists at her sides. It rankled her how much her story with Avery was like Celeste's. She had gone to other men to try and better please the man she'd married. She felt stupid now, but couldn't give in to the emotion. It also pissed her off that she was throwing the news at Avery rather than telling Harrison first like she should have.

She lifted her gaze to lock with Avery's deceitful one. "You're right. I'm a little late to be playing the motherhood game. But I'm always going to know the actual father of my child is a thousand times more honorable than you would ever have been."

"Better him than me," Avery declared.

Doris nodded. "Yes. I feel the same. You talked your legal wife —your young, trusting wife—into sleeping with another man to cover up your slimy plans to marry her for money. Now you're treating your young wife like shit when the child she carries is as much your fault as hers. You know the real story. Celeste knows the real story. I know it too. And I'm going to help see you don't get out of doing what's right this time."

Avery laughed. "Is that your closing argument, Counselor? Well, here's mine. I may be dishonorable, but at least I'm not going home to a frigid wife every night. Celeste may act mad at me in front of you and the world, but she'll still spread her legs when I ask. She's a thousand times more woman than you ever were, Doris. All I can say is Graham must want *your money* a hell of a lot more than I did to put up with your cold body under his."

Doris made a fist and pulled back her arm, not contemplating the cost. She really couldn't deal with this level of pain only with words.

"Go ahead and swing, Counselor," Avery taunted, motioning her forward with one hand. "Come on down here and roll in the mud with the rest of us mere mortals. You're no damn better than anyone else."

Her arm went flying forward intending to plow Avery's face with her fist. Instead, she was lifted and swung away before she connected. She was spun around until she ended up face-to-face with a furious, but confused Harrison.

"You're pregnant? Why didn't you tell me?" he demanded.

Doris felt the fight drain completely out of her. "Yes. I'm sorry,

Harrison. I was waiting for the right time to tell you. I never meant for you to find out this way."

Harrison reached down and gripped both her fists in his hands. "I'm happy as hell about the baby—maybe happier than I should be not knowing how you feel about it. This doesn't surprise me because the timing between us is generally bad, except in one area. But you must understand the baby means you have to marry me now. There is no more debating, Counselor. I want our baby and you. It's only right, Doris."

"Okay," Doris said quietly. "I'll marry you, but you have to let me punch Avery at least one time."

Harrison glanced at the grinning bastard still standing behind Doris. He looked back at the anger in her gaze. There was real hurt beneath her fury. He'd dug out those vicious, hurtful roots a couple of times. He was sick and tired of Avery Vincent screwing up the woman he loved.

"Under other circumstances, I'd offer to hold the asshole down and let you beat the holy shit out of him, but that's not going to work today. Vincent deserves to be beaten, but he does not deserve to ruin the reputation of one of Falls Church's finest attorneys, now does he?"

Doris pushed against Harrison's unmoving chest only to have him capture her hands again. "Do not throw my profession at me. I don't have any damn grounds to sue the perverted bastard. It's unfortunately not illegal to be an asshole," she exclaimed, as she tried to yank her fists from Harrison's grasp.

Using both hands, he moved Doris gently to the side. Her resistance didn't make it easy. "I know, but the man's got a good point about you being a better person than that. Don't roll in the mud with him. You'll only be giving him what he wants one more time."

Avery laughed. He kept his voice soft and low as he spoke. "Wow, Graham. She's really got you hooked, doesn't she? Well, let me tell you something, her money won't keep you warm at night.

Trust me. You'll be looking for a warm body first chance you get like I did."

Harrison looked at the people gathered in the hall. His dad and Angela were standing near Celeste Vincent and Doris's sister. His father gave a single head nod. He grinned in reply before he turned to Avery.

"Just what are you insinuating about the mother of my child, Vincent? She's the hottest woman alive. It's not her fault you're a limp-dick, money-grubbing weasel. I doubt you know much about how to get a woman off."

"You're just jealous because I'm shooting blanks, Graham. Knocking up Doris will teach you to keep your johnson wrapped in the future. Now you're stuck with Ms. Frigidity until your kid comes of age. Better you than me."

Doris went still. She could knowing now that Avery actually wanted this. The bastard wanted her to lose her cool. He wanted a story to tell so he could play the part of a 'wronged man' again. Well, he wasn't going to get his way this time.

"Harrison, you're absolutely right. Avery's not worth getting worked up about. Let's go somewhere so we can talk," she said firmly.

Harrison shook his head, his face growing hot in his fury. "Add bad temper to my list of sins, Counselor, but first you might need to find me a defense attorney."

"Yeah, right. Big talk, Graham. That's all you are... big talk," Avery said, shaking his head. "I'm going to split now and let you lemmings run off the nearest cliff."

The man had the nerve to bump his shoulder as he started by. He couldn't let the challenge pass. Harrison dropped Doris's hands and reacted to the posturing without stopping to think about their audience gasping in shock around him.

He grabbed Avery Vincent and slung him back against the wall he'd just vacated. Ignoring the stunned look on Vincent's face, he drew back his arm. He threw one sharp punch and the bastard crumpled to the floor. Harrison stood over him breathing hard as he stared down at the swearing man with a bleeding nose.

"If you get up, I'm dragging your ass outside this building to finish what I started. Don't insult Doris again. In fact, stay the hell away from her. That was a gentleman's tap and the last warning you're ever going to get from me. I love her and you damn well will respect her when I'm around."

Doris was breathing hard herself when she stepped to Harrison's side. She reached down and lifted his still clenched hand. "Damn it, Harrison. Did you hurt your hand on Avery's face? I told you he wasn't worth losing your temper over."

Harrison turned hot eyes in her direction. His mouth twitched when he saw mischief twinkling in her gaze. "It didn't hurt much. The man's got a glass jaw. Look—I didn't even split my knuckles. All that blood on my hand is his."

Doris smiled and backed up. He followed instinctively. He looked left and right. He wanted witnesses. He met Doris's parents wide-eyed stare and winked. Her mother covered her mouth in shock. He looked back and met the gaze of the woman he loved.

"Doris Isette Pearson, will you marry me and be my wife? It's the honorable thing for you to do, Counselor. You've completely ruined my reputation. I've never been happier."

Doris crossed her arms. "*I've* ruined *your* reputation? What about *my* reputation?"

"Rock solid," Harrison assured her. "You're a known bad-ass, but you didn't throw the punch. And the baby... well, a baby is always a blessing. My grandfather is smiling down from heaven right now because I've finally found the woman I'm going to love forever."

He moved in closer. A hushed silence fell over the crowded hallway.

"Say yes and kiss me, Doris. I want witnesses so you can't back out. I'm in this for the long haul."

Doris held out a trembling hand and put it against his chest. She wanted to fall against him, to weep in relief, but she wasn't about to do any of that in front of what appeared to be everyone presently at the club.

She cleared her throat and called on her training—needing all of it to say what had to be said. "I love you too, Harrison. I'll marry you on one condition," she answered sharply.

"Name it," Harrison ordered, not hesitating now that she'd admitted she loved him. He smiled and leaned in to sniff her. "I love your work perfume. Why don't you wear it all the time?"

"Stop trying to distract me. If the baby is a boy," she began, looking over at her sister whose smile was blinding. Ruth's breakout giggling made her grin at the sexy man waiting on her to finish her demand when she turned back. "If we have a son, I want to call him *Leland*."

Harrison stepped back, stunned by the request. "*Leland?* No. Sounds like a nerd."

Doris crossed her arms again. "Like you're not a nerd? Get real. You read financials every morning. I bet your sock drawer is a testament to your borderline OCD tendencies."

Harrison turned sideways and pointed to Avery. "I just decked your ex-husband to protect your damn honor. That proves I am not a nerd."

"And Leland Graham will also not be a nerd," Doris insisted. "He'll be sexy and strong and every bit as good a man as his father is."

Harrison bent his head and rubbed his nose. "Leland. And you've got to have this name, I take it."

"Did I stutter? Yes, I said *Leland*."

Harrison laughed. He was going to love hearing that huffy, superior tone every day. "Want to take a shower with me and talk about this? I bet I could change your mind."

"No. And I'm not that easy to convince when my mind's made

up about something. You should at least know that by now. It would take at least three or four showers… maybe five."

They both snorted when both ends of the hallway gasped equally.

"Okay, this is fun, but I'm tired of providing a show," Harrison said at last, putting his arm around her shoulders. "Leland it is. You should know, though, that I'll be praying it's a girl the whole time we're waiting. Is the baby why you were getting dizzy on the golf course?"

"Yes. And we are not naming a girl Harriett—in case you were egotistical enough to go there."

Harrison winced. "I would never do that to a girl. Who would do that to their daughter? What kind of man do you think I am?"

Doris smiled at her sister as she walked by. "See? I told you it was a dumb idea, Ruth."

Her sister's giggle made her smile, and she heard Harrison laughing beside her.

The sea of people who'd come to watch now parted to let them pass through. She heard the Stantons closing rank around Celeste and thought it was about damn time. There would be hell to pay with her own parents later, but that was the least of her worries.

Before they passed out of sight, Doris glanced back down the hallway, which was rapidly emptying. No one had even offered to help Avery stand up. He was still sitting on the floor, wiping his bloody nose on his sleeve.

EPILOGUE

Eighteen years later...

"I suppose I should have seen it coming when you made me swear to name him Leland. The boy has a pitching arm most major leaguers would kill to have, but all he wants to do is go to college and study science. What kind of career is that? He's already absentminded enough."

Doris laughed. "Our daughter is the only professional sports person in the family. You need to accept that. Our son is brilliant and agile minded just like his parents. His name is not the reason Leland likes science. He likes science because his father took him to the library every time he had the simplest question that he needed answered. The boy thinks research is fun because of you. You two can spend an entire afternoon looking up things and then come home and talk about what you found forever. Neither of you ever did that with baseball."

"Baseball doesn't require thought. It requires magic," Harrison declared. "And the only reason we still go to the library is because it's more reliable than the computer. I imagine they'll make all the information electronically available eventually. Right now the good stuff is still on microfiche. It's terribly inconvenient… especially now that I have to wear these damn readers all the time."

Harrison sipped his coffee and glanced up at the new arbor he'd built three years ago. He was sad the entire time he and Leland had worked on it. His son promised the new design would withstand everything but dry rot in the wood. So far Leland had been right.

"Quit frowning. Why are you being so maudlin today? I love the new arbor. You and Leland were able to save the wisteria and the trumpet vine. Plus, this one is just as beautiful as the original," Doris said, following her husband's gaze. "You're too nostalgic over stuff. The past is not always better than the present, Harrison. I wouldn't change a single moment I've had since I met you… embarrassment and all."

Harrison narrowed his eyes as he looked across the table. "You know what's really beautiful? You're what's beautiful. I never get tired of looking at you, Doris. I never will. I'm the luckiest man in the world."

Doris tucked her head into her chest. "You say that now, but wait until you see me hanging around the house all the time. I'm finally and officially retired. I told them I would consult, but no more going to court. It's not that I can't handle the pressure any more… I just don't want to. I'll be old enough to draw social security next year, not that I will, but you know what I mean."

Harrison studied the woman he adored, looking for signs of discontent. "Maybe you need to be on the other side of the bench for a while. Do you want to run for judge next year? I'll back your campaign. Celeste told me she'd run it for you. She ran her husband's nine years ago and he's still in office."

Doris shook her head thinking about the young man who'd come forward to prove he was the father of Celeste's child. Their child was a good man who was loved by both his parents. Leland and Hugh were good friends. Hugh was only a few months older. She'd felt old when she'd first met Harrison. Now she had an eighteen-year-old son and a sixteen-year old daughter. Life was full of surprises. Sometimes you just needed to make room for them to happen.

"No, Harrison. I'm tired of practicing law. I want to relax—do something different."

"Relax? That doesn't sound like you. Sex is the only way you relax," Harrison argued. "What do you plan to do with all your spare time when you're not relaxing?"

"Besides keeping my smart-alecky husband's ass out of hot water?" Doris asked.

"I admit you do that well, but that's not a full-time job," Harrison argued.

"Says you," Doris teased, lifting her coffee in front of her smile. "If you must know every detail of my business, I thought I might teach golf at the club. They were all about the idea. I'd be giving private lessons to strapping young men like I used to. Now that's what *I* call nostalgia."

Harrison smiled, everything in him relaxing. Perfect. Her idea was perfect. "That's a grand idea, doll. I might have to take lessons again. It's been a while since you felt me up in public. I miss those days."

Doris chuckled. "I was not feeling you up. That was just a bonus. I was perfecting your swing."

"You were perfecting something all right. It didn't swing, though. It just pointed at you—still does."

Doris smiled. "I'm changing the subject because I don't want to have to lie to Leland and his friends about why we went back to bed at ten in the morning. Did you see our stock went up again? Intel is nearly a dollar a share now. We bought ours for pennies, Harrison. Doesn't that just astound you?"

"Yes. I expect it will continue to rise as computers develop more. We're definitely going to have to find another investment project. How about we buy a retirement home this time? We'll make it upscale and appealing to those with money. The irony is that it will probably lose more money than it ever makes, but the loss would actually help us financially. We can always sell it if we find out it's too much trouble."

Doris choked as her coffee went down the wrong way. "Wow, thinking about the future, Harrison? I'm not old and feeble yet. I kind of hope I never get like that."

Harrison shook his head. "Not for you, dummy. I was thinking of your parents. You're going to outlive me."

"Doubtful," Doris said, sighing. "Yes, I suppose that does make sense. They're getting to the point where they need full-time watching. Ruth is wringing her hands over how resistant they are to hiring help. I'm game to buy a retirement facility if you are. We've got Leland's education money too. He's got a full ride at several universities, even the two that were out of state. I don't think he's going to need help with tuition. I suppose we should buy him a car, but I'd like him to live long enough to marry and have children."

Harrison laughed. "I know. Of all the traits he had to get from me."

"I know… I've paid his speeding tickets plenty of times. Leland drives like a maniac too," Doris finished.

Harrison shook his head. "Well, you won't have to worry about him marrying. The boy's already in love. He's just fighting it. But I bet you he'll pick the same college April Lansing attends. He'll make the education work so he can keep an eye on her and her dating habits."

Doris smiled. "I won't argue with that assumption because I believe you are correct." She sighed and sipped. "He's going to break her heart, though, isn't he?"

Harrison nodded. "Probably. He likes girls, but he doesn't

appreciate them. When he wises up, though, I do know he'll never stray from her."

"Because of the Graham curse?"

"Exactly. Not really a curse, though. I've loved every minute of finding you."

Doris laughed when her husband scooted his chair close to hers and kissed her neck. "I hope if Leland has a son, they name him Harrison Walter Graham II. You deserve someone to carry on your name."

Harrison slipped his arm around the woman he loved. "Is the world ready for another Harrison Graham?"

Doris giggled as she tucked her head into her husband's shoulder. "No, of course not. We'll call him Walter. With that kind of reliable name, he can be anything he wants. Walter will be a Renaissance man."

"I love you, Doris. You're going to be a great grandparent when little Walter comes along. I'm glad I'm going to get to watch."

"I love you too, Harrison. You're the best man I've ever known. I hope your grandson grows up to be just like you. Maybe then you'll forgive Leland for being a nerd like his mother."

"Okay, you've got a deal. Want to take a shower with me?"

"Do you really think that will work after eighteen years?" Doris asked.

Harrison laughed. "Doll, I'd bet every cent I own on it."

"Must be serious if you're willing to put up cold hard cash. Come on inside. I wouldn't want you to lose any of your hard earned money just because your wife wouldn't put out."

"Oh, she'll put out for me. I know how to convince her."

Harrison kissed her until she let him pull off her shirt. They had reached the patio door before his wife realized she was standing naked in the stark daylight. Doris hadn't bothered with a bra that morning.

Grinning, he followed his screeching, swearing wife to their bedroom.

—THE END—

To hear about future releases in the *Never Too Late series* and get news about all my contemporary romances, **join my mailing list**.

KEEP READING in this ebook to read an excerpt *Never Is A Very Long Time* from a new contemporary series.

NEVER IS A VERY LONG TIME

THE PERFECT DATE, BOOK 1

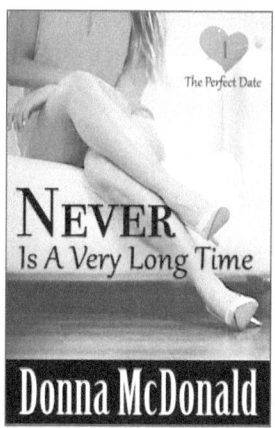

THE PERFECT DATE SERIES

The essence of all romantic comedy is that falling in love and navigating an unexpected romance is never easy or simple. Instead, it's messy and emotional, and if you're lucky, it's also sexy and fun.

Some relationship professionals, like my character of Dr. Mariah Bates in this series, sincerely want to help people find their perfect love match. For the feisty heroines I've created, many of whom are older, Mariah's going to need all the help she can get. Or maybe she just needs to step out of the way. You can be the judge.

NOTE ABOUT THE HEAT LEVEL: Not being a fan of the word "clean" when applied to romance, I will instead say the heat level in this new series is in the 1-2 range, rather than 3-4 like some of my others. The focus is on sensuality and I've packed a lot into these stories.

BOOK DESCRIPTION

Cupid she's not—but she's pretty darn close.

Nothing in the world feels better than finding her clients the perfect date. Of course finding one for herself might be nice, but creative bill paying is for college students—not for accomplished doctors in their forties. Satisfied customers keep the electricity on.

But wait, according to all the magazines the forties are the new twenties. Now if only she felt twenty...

Everything in Dr. Mariah Bates' life was perfectly fine until the moment she quit her celebrity radio job to start a dating business. Two years, a cheating ex, and a very ugly divorce later, she's suddenly homeless and living with her mother. Not exactly how she'd envisioned her life working out. Not that her mom isn't great, but come on.

With her cop ex-husband doing everything he can to ruin her business, she's at her wit's end. Throw in another cop who makes her believe in love at first sight—or at least lust—and life is a mess. Interesting, fun and tummy tingling, but a mess. Especially since another cop is the last thing she needs.

Despite a very persistent, want-to-be beau who insists he's protecting her, it's time for Mariah to take control of the game her ex has been playing. Punt or pass, she's due for a touchdown.

Everyone deserves the perfect date—even her.

CHAPTER 1

MARIAH FLINCHED AS THE WOODEN GAVEL HIT THE BLOCK IN FRONT of the judge.

"I'll hear from the defendant's attorney now."

Beside her, Bill rose and nodded once to recognize the judge's request.

"Your Honor—not to denigrate the fine work done by most detectives in our local police precincts, but the charges brought by my client's ex-husband, Detective Luray, are not backed by anything of substance. Dating services are a dime a dozen these days… no offense to my own client… but I'm having a hard time figuring out the grounds for the illegal solicitation charge the Prosecuting Attorney's office is attempting to press."

Mariah saw the judge look past her attorney to her. She was frowning and all but glaring. Dan wanted her to suffer for divorcing him and it looked as if he was actually going to get his way.

"Thank you, Counselor. Now I believe I'd like to hear your client's own defense of the charges against her," the judge declared.

"Yes, Your Honor." Bill leaned in. "Tell her your story, Mariah."

Mariah stood. "Your Honor, my name is Dr. Mariah Bates. I have a PhD in Psychology from Johns Hopkins. I am a licensed and certified marriage and relationship therapist. For over twenty years, I did a call-in radio show that helped people with their relationship issues. Now my primary business is an elite, professional dating service that is really more like a matchmaking service for busy professionals. We're a bit like Kellerher International, which is widely known, and as far as I know, quite well respected."

"If I might interject..." the prosecutor said loudly. "Dr. Bates's business does not offer access to a dating database of potential matches nor does she offer anyone a phone app as do most services of her kind. Nothing discovered in her business model indicates she is offering any ongoing match service, but rather she is selling individual time spent with a client to yet another client. It is reasonable to conclude that her business model is a potential cover for nefarious escort activities."

Mariah felt her jaw tighten. There had been no discovery at all. No one had subpoenaed her records. No, Dan had given the Hamilton County prosecutor all that misinformation. But who was going to doubt one of Cincinnati's finest?

"We charge a flat fee per service which translates in most cases to a flat fee per date. The person we find the match for pays the fee, especially if there is a pressing need, such as a business function, wedding, or other social gathering where the client feels it would be best to have a companion at his or her side. We are not following the subscription model because of discretion. This is the same reason we don't use anything like an app. Our clients are CEOs, local celebrities, sports figures, and have other high profile jobs. We work to protect the privacy of every client we help."

She turned her head to the man seated several rows behind her wearing a very expensive suit she'd bought for him five years ago. It was easier today to ignore how good Dan looked in it. Her bitterness over his actions had torn away the rose colored glasses she normally viewed him through.

"As I have repeatedly told my ex-husband, Detective Daniel Luray, the way I bill is not proof of solicitation. Instead, it provides me a reasonable cash flow to continue serving my clients. Fostering twenty-two weddings among clients last year could be used as proof of my matchmaking success, if such proof is necessary. My clients are business people who would not appreciate their carefully selected date being called an "escort" for no good reason other than Detective Luray's unfounded suspicions or his desire to get back at me for having had the nerve to divorce him."

The judge looked at the prosecutor. "Is there any real evidence against Dr. Bates's company? Any client claiming they paid for sex and didn't get any? Anybody saying they're being pimped out by Dr. Bates?"

"Not yet, Your Honor, but…"

She didn't allow the prosecutor to waffle any further. The judge's gavel hit her wooden block. "Case dismissed due to lack of evidence. Dr. Bates, we are sorry to have wasted your time this morning."

"Thank you, Your Honor," Mariah said, breathing out at last.

Bill reached over and hugged her. "You could have mentioned me and Abby, you know. We're proof of your success and you didn't even have the agency then."

Mariah shook her head. "Dan's vendetta against me is no reason to drag my friends down into the mud. It's bad enough he has me wrestling around with him in it."

She gathered up her things and moved to walk out. Bill walked closely behind. She should have guessed it wasn't going to be that easy.

"One day I will get what I need for evidence, Mariah. I'm going to be watching your ass very closely," Dan warned as she walked by him.

"Great news. Kiss my ass while you're back there nosing around," Mariah ordered, striding away from the man she had loved forever but now loathed.

Behind her, she heard Bill say something to Dan, but it was probably best she not know what passed between the two men. All of her friends had taken her side in the divorce when her long time, nice husband had suddenly turned into an ass just because she quit a lucrative job to start a more risky one. Their loyalty to her had gotten even stronger after the divorce was final and Dan was seen around town with some yet to be named bleached-hair blonde on his arm.

Mariah huffed because crying over the sad state of her love life was out of the question. She was beyond emotional hurt now. That kind of hurt had come when she went off the air and decided to do something different because she needed to feel alive and not just on autopilot. The emotional hurt had come with the thousand arguments she and Dan had frequently had about their financial inequities and her earning power—the net result being a property settlement that left her literally homeless. Dan had come out of the divorce as well as any greedy, manipulating spouse ever could have. She'd come out of it stripped of half her wealth, but missing most of her dignity.

But the good news for Mariah was that the legal cords were finally all cut. That was what mattered to her these days. Now she could move forward the way she needed to. She'd been like a rabid, trapped wolf at the end of her divorce proceedings. She'd been willing to sacrifice an arm, a leg, and the nearly million dollar home she and Dan had bought with her celebrity earnings.

Setting the trumped up criminal charges she'd just faced aside, Mariah actually thought she *had* escaped. Unfortunately, Dan continued to be there on the edges of her life—still poking and prodding at a decision he thought he had some right to have an opinion about.

Why did he bother with trying to hurt her? She'd already given him the lion's share of their possessions. Her mind kept churning on the issue, but the truth was unknowable. When your once loving husband became greedy and spiteful, there was no more pretending you understood him.

When it came right down to it, there was only one thing Mariah knew for certain these days. Divorcing Dan had put her off all men for a good long while. She could only hope her own sad relationship story wasn't going to be bad for her matchmaking business.

CHAPTER 2

"Mariah?"

Mariah lifted her head from her laptop and the task she'd hoped would distract her from her woes. Dr. Della Livingston, her twenty-seven year old multi-tasking miracle who worked mostly in exchange for research data for her book, looked ready to have a meltdown. "What's wrong, Della?"

"I know you just got back from court, but there's a Detective Monroe here asking to see you. He says he was referred by someone."

"Oh, for pity's sake. I've had enough of this," Mariah said, rising from her chair.

She straightened her unfortunately super snug pencil skirt back down over her hips. Both pieces of her favorite suit had gotten tighter in the last couple of years, but it was still the best one she owned. That was why she'd chosen it to wear to court. The light shade of rose flattered her blonde complexion without looking too feminine.

Mariah marched to the door of her office. Taking one more deep breath, she moved by a still cringing Della, until she was standing in front of the still seated man. She glared down at him. "What can I do for you, Detective Monroe?"

To her annoyance, the man's face blushed crimson just at hearing her tone. His gray eyes briefly dropped down to her legs, but they didn't linger there long, before returning to her face. Good thing too. With that much gray at his temples, the man damn well ought to know better.

"Is that how you typically greet your prospective clients?" he managed to choke out.

"No," Mariah declared flatly. "It's how I greet sleazy cop buddies of my detective ex-husband who think they're going to come around and dig into my business for no good reason. The charges were dismissed today due to lack of evidence. You've got a lot of damn nerve showing up here."

"Uh... that's not why I came," he stammered out. Then his brow furrowed. "Who's your detective ex?"

"Don't waste my time with inane questions," Mariah ordered. She watched him reach up and run a nervous hand thorough his perfectly cut hair. Had the man really believed she'd accept his lame story? It would be just like Dan to plant someone as a client here to spy for him. Well, she was not buying this new detective's innocent act.

The man cleared his throat and stood, towering above her by a good foot or more even in her heels. Her gaze traveled up to his now pained-filled gray eyes. She glared until he finally looked away from her.

"I believe I made a mistake in coming here. Elliston said you were... well, it doesn't matter. Sorry to have bothered you."

"Elliston?"

"McElroy," he said tightly. "Geeky nephew of mine. Said you were fixing him up with the perfect woman."

Hands that had been fisted on her hips dropped to her side. "I will neither confirm nor deny to you that anyone is or is not a client of my business. Privacy is not just a buzz word I throw around. However, I appreciate all referrals. If this was an honest one, I'm sorry for jumping to wrong conclusions."

He studied her for a few long moments and Mariah let him get by with it. The silence helped to calm her.

"Bad day?" he asked.

Mariah nodded. Why not confess? If the man was lying to her, Dan had already told him anyway. "Nothing life changing, but I had to go to court this morning. The experience left me a little less trusting of anyone with the first name of *Detective*."

"I caught the gist of that in your greeting. Ex causing you problems?"

"Let's just say I'm not at my best at the moment, so this unfruitful conversation can end."

His almost bashful smile over her defensiveness did strange things to her insides. What she felt in the lower regions of her body made her mad at herself. However, if he truly was Elliston McElroy's uncle, she needed to be polite.

"Let's start again." Mariah put out her hand to shake. "I'm Dr. Mariah Bates—the owner, CEO, and general doer of every role here at *The Perfect Date*."

He stared at her hand for a split second longer than proper, then swallowed her hand with his own extremely large one. He didn't shake it so much as hold it for a moment. Mariah had to stop herself from wiping her hand on her skirt when he let go. "What can I do for you, Detective?"

"First name's actually John—not Detective," he said, correcting her. "And I'm thinking coming here really wasn't the best idea. Can we just pretend I wasn't here at all?"

Mariah rolled her eyes and drew in a breath. "Look, Detective Monroe…"

"John…" he corrected again.

Mariah sighed. "Look… *John*… normally I'd sit out here and talk you into feeling a certain comfort level before coaxing you into my office for a more private chat. Seeing as how I've already yelled at you and accused you of many things you profess to be innocent of…"

"Well, I…"

Mariah held a hand up. "No, no. That's quite okay. If I'm wrong, I'm wrong. I absolutely don't want you to dash away and tell the person who referred you that I was blatantly unkind. I normally am not unkind. I'm normally quite pleasant and supportive."

Mariah fought back a sigh when his grin made a single dimple on one side of his face. His gray eyes lit with amusement. All in all… he was quite handsome.

"Unkind?" John asked. "Is that a new way of saying you tried to hand me my balls over something some other guy did to you?"

"Yes, and you're a very wise man for understanding. Please accept that this is a rare, rare day in my otherwise drama-free life," Mariah answered.

"Sure. I promise I will never tell anyone you were unkind to me," John promised softly, grinning still.

"Good. I wish you'd change your mind then. If you stay and talk to me, I promise to do my best to find your perfect date."

Head down and grinning even wider, John shook his head as he walked to the door. He raised his gaze to meet hers as he prepared to leave.

"I bet you could find her easier than you know. Good day, Dr. Bates. Maybe we'll run into each other again. Maybe I'll find my balls and come back. Anything is possible."

Mariah chuckled and felt her face heat. Lord, what had she done now? "I'll be more gentle with you next time," she promised, shocked to hear the flirty statement escape her mouth.

Laughing for real, John exited. Mariah turned to go to her office and saw Della still staring at the door. "What are you pondering, Dr. Livingston? The fact that I screwed up with a potential client, or the fact that I just went nova on a man in front of you?"

Della shook her head. "Actually, I was wondering how in the space of five minutes you went from yelling at Detective Monroe to flirting with him. Also, I'm 99.9% confident he started the flirting part of the exchange with his balls comment. I feel like I should be taking notes, but I wouldn't know where to catalog what just happened."

Mariah waved a hand. "What you witnessed was two mistakes clearing up awkwardly. Detective Monroe was never going to let me help him find a woman. Which is just as well because I'm not sure I could have matched up a still working detective without advising the woman to run away as fast as her legs could move. It's oddly fortunate that I ran him off because now I don't have to worry about my conflict of interest. It was a fairly charming end to a less than charming problem."

Della chuckled. "I'm pretty sure that was a beginning, not any kind of end."

Rolling her eyes at her young assistant's dreamy gaze, Mariah headed back to her office.

Should she tell her last client of the day that his alleged uncle had come by to see her? No, of course not. What if the man hadn't revealed his intentions to his nephew? There was no reason to compound her professional sins.

Pushing away thoughts of the grinning John Monroe, whoever he really was, Mariah studied the man leaning forward in his seat. He sighed at nearly every picture he saw.

"Problem with my choices for you, Mr. McElroy?"

Elliston McElroy, a successful entrepreneur who made software apps for a living, didn't answer her question immediately. He lifted and held up his swiping finger briefly before returning to his task of looking through the women on the tablet she'd handed him.

According to his worksheet, Elliston was five-foot ten, but he carried himself like he was six-foot eight, a family trait probably since the uncle was over six-foot tall. His close-cropped, light brown hair was gelled to stand straight up on top. The spiked hair, along with the tribal tattoos running down both forearms to his hands, created a European Soccer team look. Despite the faddishness, he pulled off the dress clothes he wore well. The sleeves of his well-made pressed cotton shirt were rolled casually to his elbows, no doubt to show off the tats. Mariah thought his thirty-two year old character was mostly revealed in the clear, blue-eyed gaze he turned her direction just before he spoke.

"Please call me Elliston. I can't handle the mister stuff. The women you picked for me are all very beautiful," he said at last.

Mariah shrugged. "We do mini-makeovers to help each client present their best for our catalogue. It helps that most work out and keep themselves maintained. I often tell male clients that we enhance female clients for presentation purposes only. Most do look a lot like their photos. I find people don't like physical surprises in dates."

Elliston sighed again.

"You're sighing very heavily, Elliston. What's wrong with them?" Mariah prompted.

His grin over her understanding was very arresting because his real masculine beauty showed up in it. Any woman would be thrilled to see that smile on his face every time she came into view. Elliston wasn't classically handsome with all those lean angles to his face, but he had that something special that made a woman want to stare at him until he snatched her up and kissed her senseless.

Now it was her turn to sigh. Mariah took her mild awareness of his maleness as a healthy sign in herself and a great sign for being able to find him someone.

Elliston slid the tablet back across the desk. "They're all my age or younger. They're like the women on all the dating sites. And I'm sure they're all very nice."

"They are," Mariah agreed. "I make sure of that."

Elliston nodded. "I guess I was hoping to find a little more maturity in my potential matches."

Mariah laughed before she could stop herself. She covered her mouth with her hand, but his narrowing gaze said she'd been caught indulging. The last thing she needed was to alienate a client with her oddball sense of humor. She was messing up as badly with Elliston as she had with his alleged uncle, John Monroe. She tamed her smile and cleared her throat.

"Am I to understand that you want me to find you someone who is older than you are?" Mariah asked to confirm.

Elliston nodded. "Yes. I think I do want that." He waved a hand at the tablet. "I've dated them already. They want a house, babies, and they get aggressive when they find out I have enough money to give that to them immediately. My perfect date is not that kind of woman. Mine is someone who just wants dinner and the pleasure of my company. That's harder to find than you might think. That's why I came to you."

Mariah nodded. "No, no. I quite believe you. However..." she paused for effect, "you need to know that mature women want things just as passionately as younger women. They just want different things than a house and babies. They want things like serious attention and utmost respect. How long is your attention span, Elliston? An older woman will demand you give her a lot of it. At the risk of being too blunt, that includes any time spent in bed."

Elliston favored her with his grin again. It really was one of his most appealing qualities. Mariah couldn't help but return it.

"I'm a great team player. I'm sure she and I can design a relationship that suits us both. The bed stuff is down the line anyway. Bed partners, like beautiful women, are easy to come by. Finding someone worth talking to is the bigger challenge."

Mariah chuckled softly. "Okay then. You've convinced me your request is sincere. Give me a couple of days to comb my database again. What's your *maturity* ceiling on age?"

He shrugged one shoulder. "I don't know. I'm pretty open-minded. What's the oldest woman in your database?"

Laughter again slipped right out of her mouth. If she wasn't so jaded, she might consider putting herself on Elliston's list. He was so... what was the word she searched for... *refreshing?* Yes, his attitude was refreshing.

"My oldest client is sixty-five and would not be a good match for you. She's a racing engineer who likes to go bungee jumping and zip lining through forests. She hates to read and watch TV. You two would never work. There would be no quiet dinners and pleasant conversations."

Elliston's answering laughter had that masculine grin permanently attaching itself to his face. "I don't know..." he teased.

Mariah shook her head. "I'll keep my recommendations for you to women under forty-five. That two decade mark is a hard dividing line. Even one decade can be a serious challenge."

"Challenge I can handle," Elliston said. "Being bored to death is my problem."

"No one I match you with will be boring," Mariah promised.

Elliston nodded. "How fast..." he paused and looked guilty. "I know this isn't like just drawing a random numbered person out of your data. But the fundraising gala is two weeks from now and..." he waved to the tablet. "I really don't want to have to take one of them. The place will be swarming with eligible bachelors from the tri-state. I'd like the woman I'm with to at least look like she's paying attention to me."

Insecurity, Mariah thought, as she nodded. It was something everyone struggled with until they met that one person who saw only them. Now it was her turn to sigh. Maybe she wasn't as jaded as she thought.

"I'm going to work on this today and tomorrow. Hopefully, I'll have some more choices for you by Friday."

"I don't mind any extra costs you have for the re-do. I just didn't know how to say what I wanted before. I should have been more open from the start," Elliston said.

"Yes. Open is good. I highly appreciate a man with an open mind and an open wallet," Mariah joked. "So let me get back to this and I'll get back to you as soon as I have some options."

CHAPTER 3

"Here. I made you some hot tea with chamomile. It won't iron out those worry lines crossing your barely forty year old face, but it might settle down those jingling nerves of yours. You're muttering to yourself again, Mariah. I heard you all the way in the kitchen."

She lifted the mug from the serving tray and sipped. No dainty cups in her mother's household. "Thanks, Mom."

"You're welcome. Now when are you moving out? Someone as successful as you are shouldn't be consigned to living in this tiny patio home with me. I know Dan left you enough cash to buy another place. I mean... you're welcome to stay, but staying with me just makes it look like that selfish prick financially took you off at the knees."

Mariah snorted at the blunt comments and at her mother's swearing. People often thought she'd gotten her bluntness from her Air Force Colonel father. That could have been the case, but it wasn't. She'd gotten it from Georgia Bates, silver-haired smart-ass extraordinaire, and possibly the best mother on the planet.

"Andrew's getting ready to take the bar next year. Did you ever tell him what his bastard of a father did—or at least tried to do—to you?" Georgia asked.

"No," Mariah said, shaking her head. "And I don't intend to. I didn't tell Amanda either. With the baby coming, she doesn't need the stress. Randy's promotion came through. They're already having to move from Long Beach to Norfolk. Amanda is full up on things to worry about. The divorce was hard enough on her. She cries every time it comes up."

Georgia sniffed. "That's baby hormones. I know you raised her to be smarter about men. In my opinion, Dan's completely redefining what being an asshole means. Criminal charges. I can't believe he did that to the mother of his children. What's really criminal is that twenty-something blonde he's boffing these days."

"Mom, please… just let it go. God knows I have. The kids don't need to be part of Dan's divorce vendetta against me. For better or worse, he's still their father."

"It's been *for worse* since you left your marriage and that's all on him. I swear that's all I'm going to say about the matter. I'm just mad. Your heart wasn't the only one he broke, Mariah. You married him so young that Dan felt like my own son. But if he'd really been my child, I would have done a lot better job raising him. I'm almost glad Ted died before this happened. He'd have gone for Dan's balls."

Her mother's words instantly made her think of John's description of what her rant did to him. Maybe she'd been channeling her father that day. Mariah relaxed only when her mother patted her shoulder.

Her father had died of a heart attack when she was a freshman in college. Her mother had grieved terribly for all the years it took her to get her PhD. Then one day her mother started living again. She'd been a terrific grandmother. She'd soon be a great-grandmother in every sense of that term. Not bad for a sharp, healthy woman in her early sixties who could out swear most men when she got angry.

"Bill was great. He practically handled it all for me. Everything got dismissed and no records will be kept of the charges. But I promise you Dan is the least of my problems at the moment. I have a couple of serious decisions to make, one of which has me stumped."

Georgia grunted. "Why? What's up? Is it anything you can discuss?"

Mariah laughed wryly. "It's no big secret, I guess. More and more young men are starting to ask for an older woman to date. This is not because they think older women are sexy or fun though. It's because they don't want to date a younger woman who wants the whole relationship package. They act like it's wrong for a woman of childbearing age to want marriage and babies. What is wrong with men these days?'

"Not a damn thing," Georgia said. "Women are the ones who've changed. A woman doesn't want to do the real work of shopping for the right guy any more. She picks one from one of those dating sites and then expects him to instantly step up to meet her relationship goals. What about genuine chemistry? What about taking the time to smile across the dinner table? It takes ten pounds of luck to find the right person. Men need time to figure things out way more than women do. Love, marriage, and family should not be a goal anyway. It's a special gift, not something to barter."

"Yes, Mom." Mariah answered simply because any complex answer would have extended the rant. "Got any friends near my age looking for the perfect man to date? Looks like I suddenly have openings for older women. Maybe I can offer them a discount to be listed."

Georgia thought for a moment. "I might. Let me think about it. How about you list them for free and let the guy pick up the tab for it. In my day, men paid their way into a woman's heart."

"I'll see if my budget can afford it," Mariah promised.

When her mother left the room, she quietly sighed in relief and went back to looking for Elliston's perfect woman.

www.donnamcdonaldauthor.com/never-is-a-very-long-time

OTHER BOOKS BY THIS AUTHOR

The Perfect Date Series
Never Is A Very Long Time
Never Say Never
Never A Dull Moment
Never Ever Satisfied
Never Be Her Hero
Never Try To Explain

Never Too Late Series
Dating A Cougar
Dating Dr. Notorious
Dating A Saint
Dating A Metro Man
Dating A Silver Fox
Dating A Cougar II
Dating A Pro

Art Of Love Series
Carved In Stone
Created In Fire

Captured In Ink
Commissioned In White
Covered In Paint

Non-Series Books
The Wrong Todd
SEALed For Life
A Secret Dare
Saving Santa
Mistletoe Madness
No ELFing Way

Visit Donna's website to see more books.

ABOUT THE AUTHOR

DONNA MCDONALD

After 35 years of doing everything for a living except writing books, Donna McDonald published her first romance novel in March of 2011. Forty plus novels later, she admits to living her own happily ever after as a full time author.

Her work spans several genres, such as contemporary romance, paranormal, and science fiction. Humor is the most common element across all her writing. Addicted to making readers laugh, she includes a good dose of romantic comedy in every book.

How To Contact Donna...
www.donnamcdonaldauthor.com
email@donnamcdonaldauthor.com